D0046870

THE GREAT WAR

STORIES INSPIRED BY ITEMS FROM THE FIRST WORLD WAR

This is a work of fiction. Names, characters, places, and incidents are either products of the authors' imaginations or, if real, are used fictitiously.

Compilation and introduction copyright
© 2014 by Walker Books Ltd.
Illustrations copyright © 2014 by Jim Kay

"Our Jacko" copyright © 2014 by Michael Morpurgo
"Another Kind of Missing" copyright © 2014 by A. L. Kennedy
"Don't Call It Glory" copyright © 2014 by Marcus Sedgwick
"The Country You Called Home" copyright © 2014 by John Boyne
"When They Were Needed Most" copyright © 2014 by Tracy Chevalier
"A World That Has No War in It" copyright © 2014 by David Almond
"A Harlem Hellfighter and His Horn" copyright © 2014 by Tanya Lee Stone
"Maud's Story" copyright © 2014 by Adèle Geras
"Captain Rosalie" copyright © 2014 by Timothée de Fombelle;
    translation copyright © 2014 by Sam Gordon
"Each Slow Dusk" copyright © 2014 by Sheena Wilkinson
"Little Wars" copyright © 2014 by Ursula Dubosarsky

All rights reserved. No part of this book may be reproduced, transmitted, or stored in an information retrieval system in any form or by any means, graphic, electronic, or mechanical, including photocopying, taping, and recording, without prior written permission from the publisher.

First U.S. edition 2015

Library of Congress Catalog Card Number 2013955699

ISBN 978-0-7636-7554-7

SCP 20 19 18 17 16 15

10 9 8 7 6 5 4 3 2 1

Printed in Humen, Dongguan, China

This book was typeset in Futura and Sabon.

Candlewick Press
99 Dover Street
Somerville, Massachusetts 02144

visit us at www.candlewick.com

THE

DAVID ALMOND • JOHN BOYNE
TRACY CHEVALIER • URSULA DUBOSARSKY
TIMOTHÉE DE FOMBELLE • ADÈLE GERAS

GREAT

A. L. KENNEDY • MICHAEL MORPURGO
MARCUS SEDGWICK • TANYA LEE STONE
SHEENA WILKINSON

WAR

illustrated by JIM KAY

STORIES INSPIRED BY ITEMS
FROM THE FIRST WORLD WAR

CANDLEWICK PRESS

What passing-bells for these
who die as cattle?
Only the monstrous anger
of the guns.

— Wilfred Owen, "Anthem for Doomed Youth"

Previous page: **CRASHED SOPWITH CAMEL**
World War I was the first conflict in which aircraft played a major role. Between 1914 and 1918, aircraft technology advanced at a remarkable rate. The Sopwith Camel, introduced in 1917, was Britain's most successful fighter plane. Camels shot down 1,294 enemy aircraft—more than any other Allied plane.

The War to End All Wars

World War I, known at the time as the Great War, was the most destructive conflict the world had ever seen. Sixteen million people lost their lives, twenty million were wounded, and millions more were left homeless and starving.

What started as a small conflict in the Balkans quickly escalated into the first truly global war. At first the leaders of the nations involved thought it would be over quickly, but the fighting dragged on for four long, bloody years, from August 1914 until an armistice went into effect at 11 a.m. on November 11, 1918.

The stories in this collection are inspired by objects from this terrible conflict. Some, like the Brodie helmet, were used in the fighting. Others, like the war-time butter dish, belonged to those left behind at home. Each story gives us a glimpse into the millions of lives that were changed by the war. Each object brings home the reality of a war that is now fading from living memory — a war many hoped and believed would be a war to end all wars.

Previous page: **ABANDONED CARTS**
Most ammunition, guns, food, and other supplies were transported to the front lines of the war in carts pulled by horses or mules. The animals struggled to move along narrow roads in bad weather, often getting bogged down by mud, and thousands were killed by shell fire.

Contents

. . . .

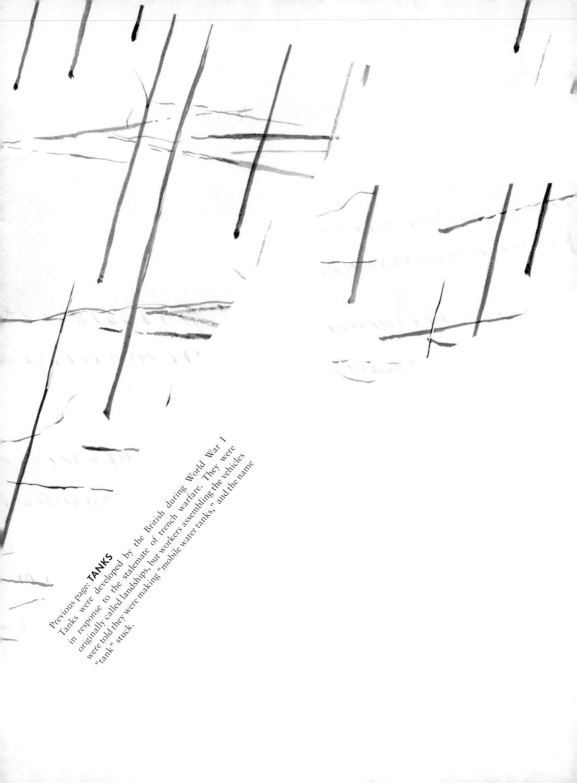

Previous page: **TANKS**
Tanks were developed by the British during World War 1 in response to the stalemate of trench warfare. They were originally called landships, but workers assembling the vehicles were told they were making "mobile water tanks," and the name "tank" stuck.

MICHAEL MORPURGO

OUR JACKO

I grew up with the tin hat. The first time I was aware of it, I was about three or four, and Otto, my big brother, was eight or nine, I suppose. Otto wore it almost constantly, not just when he was playing war games with his friends, but on his scooter, or bicycling, or sitting on the swing, even at meals sometimes—if he could get away with it. It hung by the strap on his special "Otto hook" by the back door, with his coat. It became "Otto's tin hat," and for a while it was his most treasured possession. He painted it bright red, the same red as the postman's van, and forbade me from wearing it or even touching it, threatening me with an arm twist, or death, if I did. I didn't want anything to do with it anyway. It was often the cause of quarrels between us, and we quarreled a lot in those days. From the moment he told me, gleefully, that it was the helmet of a dead soldier, I hated the sight of it. There was a hole in it where he said a bullet had gone in and "done him in." I remember his very words, remember being horrified at the time and haunted by the thought of it. I still am.

Otto liked to annoy me, to provoke me, I think. He always knew that one sure way to get me riled was to say that war was exciting, that peace was boring. Often I'd lose my temper with him, and it would end up as a shouting match — and once or twice, I'm ashamed to say, I'd find myself trying to punch him or kick him, which of course was just what he wanted. He could taunt me then. He could call me a hypocrite or "a bloodthirsty little warmonger."

In time, thank goodness, Otto tired of his tin hat and his war games. My mother used it as a feeding bowl for the hens, but that didn't work because the hens could perch on the rim of it, and the corn would spill out onto the mud and too much of it was wasted. So then we used it for collecting the eggs instead. At least with the eggs in it, resting on a soft bed of hay, I couldn't see the hole. I hated that hole.

Then, for a while, my mother rigged it up outside the porch as a hanging basket. The hole was perfect for that, she said, because the soil could drain well. It hung there by the front door for years. She grew white petunias in it that spilled over the side and cascaded down, like white tears. I would reach up and touch them for luck on my way off to school in the mornings. I liked that they were white. I liked white because it was the color of peace. It seemed right and proper that the bloodred helmet, to me so much a symbol of the cruelty of war, was now being used as a flower basket, and could scarcely be seen through the abundance of white flowers — flowers of peace.

As we grew older, Otto and I continued to argue just as passionately about war and peace. There was less name calling, and I had learned by now that I had to keep my cool if I wanted to win an argument with him. He was a great reader of books, doing history at school, and would blind me with his encyclopedic knowledge of the past. He told me, rather patronizingly, that I would soon come to understand that although war might be unpleasant — even undesirable in some ways — it was sometimes necessary politically and justifiable morally. He said grandly that it was no good my being "a bleeding-heart pacifist," that I would soon have to learn that the world was as it was, not how we would like it to be.

It was a relief to me when Otto went off to college, taking his burning ideas with him. He could stir them all up there, I thought, and leave me in peace at home.

Meanwhile, the tin hat, the original cause of all this sibling strife, had long since vanished. My mother had replaced it with a proper hanging basket, still growing petunias, still flowers of peace that brushed my face like a blessing as I walked through the front door. I liked that.

I was about fourteen when the tin hat reappeared. Had we not been moving—from one side of Stratford to the other, not far—it is likely that the tin hat would never have been seen again. My mother discovered it at the bottom of a tea chest in the back of the garage, during the big sort-out as we were packing up to leave. Otto was not there to claim it, and I would cheerfully have thrown it away along with everything else. It was Mr. Macleod, our history teacher at school, who, strangely, was responsible for saving the tin hat and for much of what happened next, too.

The day after my mother came across the tin hat in the tea chest, Mr. Macleod announced the school history trip to the battlefields of the First World War in Belgium. It would be a three-day trip and was absolutely essential for our studies, he said. In addition, because it was the centenary of the First World War, he had decided to put on a full-scale school production of a musical called *Oh, What a Lovely War!* He wanted as many students from his history class as possible to be in it, "whether you can act or not, whether you sing or not."

I went up to him after class and told him that I could not go to Belgium because it would be too expensive and I couldn't be in his play because I didn't like acting. I didn't tell him the truth, which was that I had become committed to the idea of peace and simply hated the idea of visiting battlefields and the whole subject of war. Mr. Macleod was quite dismissive and said I should think about it and that he'd speak to my mother about it.

When I got home that evening, Otto was back from college. He'd come home for the holidays, and there on the kitchen table beside the teapot was the tin hat.

"Mum said you wanted to chuck it," he said, stuffing himself with his favorite treacle cake. "That's my childhood, that tin hat. No one's chucking it."

Here we go again, I thought. "Best thing to do with it," I told him. "It belongs in the rubbish, like war does."

"Very profound," Otto mumbled, his mouth full.

And then I told them all about Mr. Macleod's plans for the school trip and the play.

"'S'all history is, one long, lousy war," I said. "I'm not going to Belgium, anyway."

That was when war almost broke out in the family, and the two of them ganged up against me.

"You should go," my mother said. "I think everyone should go at least once in their lifetime. It's part of our history, part of who we are. That war changed the world."

"Surely," Otto joined in, "if you want what you say you want—a world at peace—you have to understand the consequences of a world at war. Plenty of consequences buried out there in the battlefields of the First World War—millions of them. Just because you don't approve of it, that's no reason not to face it, however sad it makes you feel, however angry."

I didn't agree with Otto, but I listened to him. He wasn't teasing me or patronizing me. I felt he was at least taking me more seriously.

I think it was partly because of what Otto said to me, and how he said it, that I changed my mind about the school trip, and the next day I put my name down for it. But there was another reason, too, even more compelling: the strange and timely reappearance of the tin hat, Otto's old war helmet. It was still there on the kitchen table the next morning at breakfast before I went off to school. Otto wasn't up; no one was. I sat there eating my muesli and staring at the hole in the helmet. This helmet had belonged to a soldier in the First World War— a soldier who had died, a soldier only a little older than me, some mother's son, some child's father. He would be out there somewhere, buried on the battlefield. I would go.

That morning, Mr. Macleod asked us to do some research when we got home. "Go online," he said. "Have a look at your family tree. Dig around a bit. Ask your mum and dad, grandparents, aunties, uncles. Do you have a relative, a great-great-grandfather, who was a soldier or a sailor, or in the Royal Flying Corps maybe? Did they die in the war somehow, or did they come home? Do you have a great-great-grandmother who was a nurse at the front or who worked in a munitions factory? Bring in anything you can find. Old photos, medals, badges, letters. We'll put an exhibit together. We want to look into the faces of those who lived then, read their words, hear their voices, as far as we can. We want to know how it was to be them, to live through those times. They were there. They can tell us."

I had never known Mr. Macleod to be so passionate, so inspiring. He was, I had always thought, a bit of a dry old stick. I could see—we all could—that this wasn't simply dusty old history for him. He wanted each of us to go with him on a voyage of discovery into the past, so that, as he put it, "we can better understand our present and make a better future. It's what those millions of 'the mouthless dead' would have wanted."

When I got home that evening and told everyone about the exhibit, I was amazed at Otto's response. I'd never seen him like this, so interested and helpful. He said at once that our tin hat had to be "the star of the show." He wasted no time and set about removing the red paint so that it wouldn't look like a kid's toy anymore. He said it should be khaki again, its proper color, its original color. It didn't take him long. The toxic odor of paint stripper filled the house all evening.

But my mother wasn't at all sure about it. "We don't really know it's a helmet from the First World War," she said. "It could be from the Second World War—they looked just about the same, didn't they?"

At that, my father turned the television off and sat up, suddenly taking notice. "No, no," he said. "It's definitely First World War. Belonged to Grandpa Tom's grandfather. Jacko. We always called him Our Jacko in the family when I was growing up. That's what I was always told when I was little: that Our Jacko didn't come home, but his helmet did. Brought home by his best friend. That's how come we got it."

"But that could just be a story, couldn't it?" my mother said.

"No, no. There's a photo of Our Jacko somewhere," my father replied, getting up. "I remember it. And some other stuff Grandpa Tom left us. Haven't seen hide nor hair of it for years. There was a couple of medals, too, if I remember right, and a book, a little notebook full of writings you couldn't hardly read, so I never did. And yes, there was a shell case, made of brass or metal or something. Mum used to polish it up and put flowers in it. She always called it Our Jacko's vase. But it wasn't a vase, not really. Grandpa Tom always told me it was a shell case that belonged to Our Jacko, and came back with his helmet and things."

"What happened to it?" my mother asked.

"Well," said my father, "so far as I know, it was all in an old leather suitcase. We had it up in the attic once—I know we did."

My mother looked suddenly aghast. "I threw it away this morning," she said. "Thought it was empty."

We retrieved the suitcase at once and opened it up on the kitchen table. It smelled of mold and decay. At first it looked as if it was full of nothing but old Christmas decorations—paper stars, a plastic angel, a Santa without a head, some glitter balls, and a wooden crib—but underneath all these long-forgotten remnants of Christmases past lay what looked like a large metal vase.

"See?" said my father. "That's it—that's the shell case." He held it up.

Otto took it from him to get a closer look. "Look, Dad, it's got an engraving on it, and writing too! Can't hardly read it. Too grimy. It looks like a shell case, all right. Must be. And Grandma used it for flowers! Weird or what?"

"No, it's not weird," I said. "That's the best thing it could be used for. She was turning a weapon of war into a flower vase."

But they weren't listening to me. Hidden away under more Christmas decorations, my mother had found a large brown envelope. She gave it to my father. He opened it and took something out.

"It's here," he said. "The notebook." He turned to the first page and read out loud: "*This book belongs to Lt. Jack Morris, actor, Shakespeare Memorial Theatre, Stratford-upon-Avon.* That's Our Jacko! It's got a title: *In my mind's eye. Thoughts of home, some poems I know and love.*" He turned the notebook over and looked at the back. "It says, *To whoever may find this, please return it to the theater in Stratford, where I work; or to Ellie, my dear wife, and to Tom, our little son, at Mead Cottage, Charlecote Road, Hampton Lucy. I should be forever grateful. Lt. Jack Morris, Sherwood Foresters. Ypres, Belgium.* It's his writing, Our Jacko's handwriting, from a hundred years ago," my father said, in a whisper almost.

At that moment, something fell out of the notebook and onto the table. I picked it up. It was a photograph. A young man in uniform stood there, hand resting on a table beside him, stiff and stern, looking at me out of his black-and-white world. Looking me straight in the eye, knowing—I could see it—that he was going to die, that he was telling me so, too. He looked more like a boy dressing up than a soldier.

"Here," my father went on, handing the notebook to Otto, "you read it. It's in pencil. I can't read it too well."

Otto began to read in a hushed voice. We all listened.

"*June 18, 1915*
Dearest Ellie,

I hope one day, when all this is over, to come home and bring this little notebook with me. Should it come home without me, then you will know forever how much you and little Tom are in my thoughts; you, and the walks we went on down the river, and the poems we loved to read together. I will write nothing of this place or of the war. It is a nightmare that one day I shall wake from and then forget. And if I don't wake, then you shall never know. I don't want you ever to know.

I want only to write of the good times, to see them and you again in my mind's eye; to read them again and again, to remind me that there is goodness and beauty and love in this world, to remind me of you and of our Tom."

Otto paused for a moment, and then read on:

"*Our first walk together:*

In my mind's eye . . . I am walking down through the meadows along the river beyond Half Moon Spinney, where I walked when I was a boy, where I walked with you, Ellie, where one day you and Tom and I will all walk together, and I will pick a buttercup and hold it under his chin to see if he likes butter or pick a dandelion clock and puff on it to tell the time.

It is best as it is now in the early morning, the cows wandering legless through the mist. I am alone with them and with birdsong. I am walking where Will Shakespeare walked, where he fished, where he dreamed the dreams of his plays and his poems, along the bank where he sat and wrote, maybe. A kingfisher flew for him, too, and it flew for us once — do you remember, Ellie? As it flies for me now, in my mind's eye. Straight like an arrow on fire out of the mist. And a heron lifts off, unhurried. Heron, kingfisher, they were both taught to fish as I was, by their fathers — and mothers — and I shall teach Tom, when I come home. The river flows slow now, in gentle eddies, unhurried. She's taking her time. The aspen trees are quivering in the breeze. The whole world along the river trembles with life."

No one spoke, not for a long time. Otto was turning the pages of the notebook.

"There's lots of them, lots of walks along the river, all in his mind's eye," he said. "That's how he begins each walk. That's Shakespeare, isn't it? I did it at school. That's from *Hamlet*. And then there's poems, lots of them. I think they're Shakespeare, too. He must have learned them as an actor. He's written them all down. Listen:

Over hill, over dale,
Through bush, through brier,
Over park, over pale,
Through flood, through fire.
I do wander everywhere
Swifter than the moon's sphere . . ."

"We've been to the theater in Stratford, haven't we?" said my mother. "We've been where he acted. Can I see?" She took the book from Otto and looked through it. "All the poems he loved most, and all the walks he loved, and the people he loved," she said. "And all in this little book. All the good in his life in this book."

My mother continued reading the notebook. Occasionally she would read from another walking episode or poem.

"He knew the river like the back of his hand," she said. "All the flowers and all the birds. All the places we know, too. He was there! Listen to this."

From each excerpt she read out, we learned a little more about Our Jacko. He had done a lot of falling in love, we discovered: with Shakespeare first, after he saw a play—*Henry V,* it was—in the theater at Stratford when he was twelve, and then with acting from that day on; with walking; with boating; and later, when he was older, with Ellie, who worked with costumes at the theater. He'd met her when he first acted in walk-on parts on the stage at Stratford, as a spear carrier, or a courtier, or a soldier.

I had been looking at the photo of Our Jacko all the time my mother was reading. It was as if I could hear his voice in every word. I turned the photo over. On the back was written: *Jack Morris, my husband, father of Tom, son, actor, soldier. Our Jacko. Born: September 23, 1892, Stratford. Killed: October 20, 1915, Ypres. He may have no known grave, but he rests in our hearts forever.*

We then had the most intense family discussion I can ever remember, about what I should or should not take in to school for the exhibit. My father said I could take in the tin hat and the shell case, but that the rest was private and too precious. I argued that no one had thought the notebook precious when it had been stuffed away in an old envelope for years.

It surprised me how adamant my father was about it — but I was even more surprised when Otto piped up in my defense.

"The photo and the notebook may be precious and unique and irreplaceable," he said, "but they tell Our Jacko's story. Everyone should know his story."

And he came up with a solution: we would photocopy the photo and all the pages of the notebook.

The tin hat was already khaki again, hardly a fleck of red paint to be seen, thanks to the paint-stripping job Otto had done. Now he took on the cleaning of the shell case. Within an hour or so, the tarnish of a century was rubbed and polished away. It shone now; it gleamed. The engraving turned out to be of flowers all around—poppies, they looked like—and above them was a name: *Ypres*. The place where Our Jacko had been killed, the place where I was going on my school trip to the battlefields.

On the bottom of the shell case, the writing, now quite legible, told us more about when and where it was made: *1915. Patronefabrik. Karlsruhe.* My father thought Karlsruhe must be the name of a German town. We googled it to be sure. He was right.

"Same year, isn't it?" said Otto. "The year Our Jacko was killed. This was a German shell, fired in Ypres."

No one said anything.

Later that evening, I was alone with my mother in the kitchen. There was a song playing on a CD, one of her favorites, which I was fed up with hearing—I knew it too well. She was singing along with it:

"All around my hat I will wear the green willow,
And all around my hat . . ."

As she was jigging to the rhythm, I happened to look out the window at the window box where she grew her tulips, always white—she loved white tulips. Somehow the words of that song and the white of the tulips wove themselves into an idea that fast became a plan, and one I was very soon determined to carry out. But it wasn't just the tulips and the song that made up my mind; it was the thought of Our Jacko dying so young, only twenty-three, who had walked the banks of the river where I walked, acted in the theater I had been to, who never came home, who had no known grave, who never walked the riverbank again with Ellie or Tom.

I took the notebook up to bed with me that night and read it from cover to cover, following in my mind's eye where he had walked, seeing his face in my head with every word. Every walk he wrote about, every poem he wrote down, made me more certain I was doing the right thing.

I was up early before the others. After quite a search, I found the ribbon I was looking for in a drawer in the kitchen and took the tulips I needed from the window box. By the time I got to school, the trestle tables for the exhibit were up in the library, covered in Union Jacks from end to end. Mr. Macleod was busying himself making a comprehensive list of all the items brought in. There were medals—lots of those; buttons and badges; one or two sepia photographs; something that looked like a garden hoe but that he said was a trenching tool; and a large photo Mr. Macleod had discovered himself, he told me, of children from our school, taken in front of the old building. Some of the boys were in sailors' uniforms; the girls were in smock dresses; all were hollow-cheeked and unsmiling, all wearing big hobnail boots.

"That was taken in 1914," he told me. "Twenty-three of them went. Eight never came back. Him . . . him . . . him. And her, too . . . She was killed in a zeppelin raid on London, where she had gone to live with her auntie. What've you brought in, then?"

But before I could tell him, he was distracted by the head teacher.

It didn't take me long to put out our family items. I found some water for the shell case and arranged the white tulips. I tied the white ribbon around the tin hat, leaned the photo of Our Jacko up against the shell case, and placed the notebook beside it. Then I wrote on the labels Mr. Macleod had provided:

Lt. Jack Morris. Sherwood Foresters. Son, husband, father, actor at Stratford, soldier. Killed 1915, Ypres.

Beside the tin hat, I propped up the card on which I had written out the poem the evening before in bed:

All around his hat
I will wear the white ribbon,
All around his hat
For a twelvemonth and a day.
And if anyone should ask me
The reason I am wearing it,
It's all for Our Jacko,
Who's far, far away.

We went to Ypres a few weeks later. We saw the museum there—In Flanders Fields, it's called. I'd never cried in a museum before. We stood in windswept war cemeteries, walked along the lines of gravestones, read the names, saw how young they were, how many there were. Thousands upon thousands. Mr. Macleod took us to the place where the Christmas truce of 1914 had taken place, where both sides had met in the middle and exchanged gifts, played a game of soccer, and sung carols. He showed us where the trenches must have once been, the wire, the shell holes. We were standing in no-man's-land, he said. Some of us sang songs from *Oh, What a Lovely War!* I had decided, after finding out that my great-great-grandfather Our Jacko had been an actor, that I wanted to be in the play after all. We sang "When This Lousy War Is Over" and "They Were Only Playing Leapfrog" and "Good-bye-ee."

On our last evening, we went to hear the bugles played under the Menin Gate, where they play them every evening. We stood there with hundreds of others, the bugles echoing under the great arch, and as they played, I looked upward to where the sound was rising. And as I looked, I read the names, each one like Our Jacko, a son, a husband maybe, a father maybe. I saw his name without even looking for it, as if he were showing me. *Jack Morris, Lt.* He was there in among all the other thousands of those who had no known grave.

As the last echoes of the bugles died away, I knew what I had to do, what I felt Our Jacko was telling me to do.

I got home. I talked to Otto about it, asked what he thought—and I'm glad I did, because he came with me the next day, the tin hat in his backpack, as we followed in Our Jacko's footsteps all the way from Hampton Lucy to Stratford along the river, as far as we could. We stopped from time to time as he had done, maybe where he had, and read from his notebook to each other. And we ended our journey in a rowing boat, as we knew he and Ellie had done so often together, and then walked through the gaggle of ducks and geese, up the steps into the theater.

Otto said I should do the talking because it had been my idea. The problem was finding the right person to talk to. I think we must have looked rather bewildered and lost, because in the end, as luck would have it, the right person found us. She was, she told us, the "front-of-house manager." I had no idea what that meant, but it sounded important, so I told her why we had come.

"Well, you see," I began, "our great-great-grandfather, Our Jacko—Jack Morris, really—was an actor here in 1914, and he was killed in the war, and our great-great-grandmother worked here, too, in the theater. She did the costumes, and that's how they met. And we saw *Henry V* here once, like Our Jacko did, too, and the soldiers wore hats in it, tin hats like this one."

I took the tin hat out of the backpack and showed it to her. "This is Our Jacko's helmet from the First World War, and I thought—we thought, Otto and me—that it belongs here, so maybe one day it can be used in a play. Because Our Jacko loved acting, loved Shakespeare, loved the theater."

I held it out to her and she took it, and then for many moments she stood there, looking down at it and saying nothing.

Then she said, "I wonder, could you wait a moment?"

So we did. We waited for quite some time before she came back and asked us to follow her. She led us through the doors into the theater itself. The stage was empty of scenery, but it was lit up, and on the stage were dozens of actors, all looking at us as we walked toward them. A couple of them helped us up onto the stage.

"Tell them what you told me," said the front-of-house manager. "The whole story."

So, with a little encouragement from Otto, I did.

When I had finished, one of the actors started to clap, then another, then all of them. And we knew they were clapping for Our Jacko and for Ellie, so Otto and I clapped, too.

We went home on the bus, silent in our thoughts, with two free tickets to *A Midsummer Night's Dream*. Otto looked over and smiled at me. I smiled back. We were happy.

Previous page: **SOLDIERS IN A TRENCH**
World War I was largely fought from entrenched positions, with fighting lines moving very little. Soldiers became ensconced in fortified trenches they had dug in the ground, facing their enemy across an area known as "no-man's-land." Trench warfare has since become a metaphor for the futility of war.

ANOTHER KIND OF MISSING

What me and my dad are fond of is the bigness down here at Frognal House. He says it's like he's the lord of the manor, sleeping in a great, huge mansion with fancy ceilings and these proper nice floors, all shiny. He says this place has rooms as big as drill halls, which is true—they're just that enormous. I saw him in his drill hall once when he was practicing to be a soldier. I climbed and looked through the window. He snapped his boots down smart and swung his Lee-Enfield rifle up and was perfect. He was like himself, only better. He was the best at everything.

A. L. Kennedy

And the parading and the coming to attention made echoes and bangs that nobody minded. At Frognal House, all the noises get bigger and bigger, as if having so much space means they'll never stop.

Dad's bed, though, isn't somewhere big—it's in an attic kind of place that can only hold four people—Parker and Hepplewhite and Barnes and my dad. There's no room for bangs and echoes, which is good, because Parker and Hepplewhite and Barnes and my dad don't like noises. Especially Barnes. Barnes isn't happy if a door slams or the rain clatters on the slates.

Once Barnes was crying when I visited, because it had been raining for lots of days, one after another. My dad said the trouble was that Barnes had been brave right across France and so he was tired now, but he would pick up shortly. Except for the clattering, the attic suits them all—it's cozy.

Some of the great, long downstairs rooms have rows of beds, beds with lots of men where there used to be one person sleeping by themselves, which must have been lonely for whoever that was—maybe some boy who was going to be a duke when he grew up. And the boy could have played in the grounds outside the buildings, which go on everywhere for almost as far as you can see. That would be lonely, too, if you were by yourself. The staff call them "grounds" because they're more than a garden; they're lots of gardens put together and then some woods—like a park. If you're a duke, you can have your own park. You'd need a compass to not get lost.

I've got a compass, so I don't get lost, not ever. My dad gave me his the first time I came—it's all heavy brass and in a leather case that used to fit on his belt, and it went everywhere with him for ages. It has his name—Arthur Buchanan—and his number, cut into the metal around the side. There's another man's name and number on the back. That man didn't need to know where he was going anymore, which is why my dad got the compass. Sometimes in the trenches there wouldn't be time for them to have new things, and they just made the best of it.

I keep the compass shined up and the safety catch on so the little needle doesn't swing and break. When I hold it and let it go and hunt out north, it bobs around like anything, like something on water, and it's hard to tell where you are or what it's saying. That's because I can't keep my hands still enough. But my dad could. He kept his hands steady all the way, and he found home.

In a while his hands will stop shaking. It's having to be so still for so long that means they move a lot for now, and I'm not to worry.

I come up the path to the hospital with the compass, and then I sight through the little notch and fix the degrees where the main house is and where Dad's got his window. I am learning how to take a bearing on trees and things, and I need a map of here, because you can do that with maps, too—you can fix headings and take bearings, and I should practice that for when there's another war and it will be useful.

Back with my mum, I sleep with the compass in its case and under my pillow. She doesn't know about it, even though it's just us there at Ford Street. She's by herself inside, and I'm by myself, too.

There was no time to make brothers or sisters, but that means I don't have to share where I sleep. I get to be lonely like a duke. Mum says I rattle around. She also says that I behave like I think I really am the Duke of Bloody Somewhere because I leave the doors open and let the heat out when the price of coal is something awful and you can hardly get it, even when you try. But my room is the right size when I'm in it, and doesn't scare me, not even if it rains and thunders.

While the war was still on, I used to keep a map on my wall of where the front line was. I made it up from what they said in the papers. It wasn't a very good map, because it had to cover lots of countries and so everything on it was very little, but me and Mum would mark it with pins and threads and guess where my dad would be, because the censorship people wouldn't let him tell us in his letters. Which was stupid. It's not like we're Germans.

We don't know any Germans. Except Mr. and Mrs. Semmelweiss, who used to run the Vienna Bakery, and they were nice people, and Mrs. Semmelweiss was born in Croydon and not a bit German, and Mr. Semmelweiss hadn't been German since he was a baby, and he wouldn't remember how. People where we live stopped buying their bread at the bakery, and Mrs. Semmelweiss stopped going out, or kept crying once she'd gone out and then coming over to our house and crying more. My dad went down the main street in his uniform then, and stood outside the shop and shouted for everyone to go inside—like he was already an officer—shouted at them whether they needed bread or not, and told them to blooming well buy something. Everyone paid attention and did what they were ordered to, because my dad in uniform looks amazing. He gets to wear a kilt like a mad Highland charger, because he's a London Scottishman. And he was only a private then, but he's a natural leader of men. People paid attention.

My dad had gone to school with Mr. Semmelweiss, who's got funny legs and used to get laughed at by the other boys. Dad said he wasn't having any more nonsense from anyone about not wanting to eat the kaiser's cakes or nothing, because the cakes weren't the kaiser's; they were London cakes, made in London with English flour, and not to be so comical. Dad went all red in the face about it, like when I cracked the parlor window playing marbles when I shouldn't have ever been in the parlor by myself and what was I thinking—redder than that, even. And when Mrs. Hopkins came along past the bakery—Mrs. Hopkins, who is horrible and throws water at our cat—and she tried to start saying Mr. Semmelweiss was bound to be a spy, my dad told her she should shut her spinstery old mouth and that she talked Welsh at home, only who knew if it really was Welsh—it might be Turkish and she could be a spy for the enemy—and that made her quiet, all right, and she scurried away back indoors after that.

And it proved what I always thought, which was that my dad and mum didn't like Mrs. Hopkins and only said I had to be polite to her because grown-ups have to be polite to everyone. Grown-ups have to be polite to everyone, but they have to shoot everyone, too. There's nothing in the middle with being a grown-up. Maybe they wouldn't have to go away and fire whizbangs and mortars at one another and get shot at if they were allowed to tell old bags how rotten they are whenever they wanted.

In the end, Mr. Semmelweiss changed the name of the Vienna Bakery to the Windsor Bakery, which was funny because a while later King George changed his name to Windsor, too, so that him and his family wouldn't sound German. They were called Sacks of Something before and he knew the kaiser and they were family and all that, but you can't help who your family is, and he's a very good king, although he's a navy man and not a soldier, which is why he's allowed to wear a beard.

People liked buying the Semmelweisses' bread once they were running the Windsor Bakery. Which my dad said proved people would try to ride a fire screen if you just one day called it a donkey, because they were mainly a thickheaded lot. There were Union flags in the bakery window, and it was busy — except for when the flour ran out — and Mrs. Semmelweiss came to see Mum less, which was a shame because she always brought us cake when she visited. She put it aside for us specially. The last time she came — which was about when Dad arrived home and was sent to the hospital — she said she was very sorry that my dad got hurt and that Mr. Semmelweiss was very sorry too and sorry that he couldn't serve, because of his funny legs, and my mum shouted at her and then hugged her, which didn't make any sense.

We've still got rationing now. The war has stopped and gone away, but there's no sugar, or not much. I don't know what they did with sugar in the fighting to use it up, but it mostly went away. Maybe it went for making plum and apple jam. Dad wrote and told us they got a lot of that in the trenches and how you could make a stove out of a jam tin. And he wrote that him and the boys called their sausages "barkers" because you never knew what was in them.

I wouldn't want to eat a dog. Not even one that was old and had died in its sleep.

Mum said after the Bakery Battle — which was my dad's name for it — that I still had to be polite to Mrs. Hopkins. Which wasn't fair. I thought then it would have been fair to shoot Mrs. Hopkins. Only in the leg or something. Not a big wound, just a tiny one, to make her be nice for a change. Shooting makes a mess, though, and I might get it wrong, so I've changed my mind about that. Dad says a man can change his mind.

But I still hate Mrs. Hopkins. She gets extra barkers from the butchers, over what her ration's supposed to be, and that should mean she gets a fifty-pound fine. She's never, ever given us a penny for the Guy on Guy Fawkes Night, not on any year, not even for Guys with a lot of work in them, not for the Guy wearing Sam Wainwright's aunt Ida's best hat, which stopped him from being allowed to play with us until after Christmas because we were all running wild without our fathers and he needed to be taught a lesson.

So Mrs. Hopkins wouldn't pay a fifty-pound fine to a policeman or the judge. I bet she's got the money, all right, because she doesn't spend anything. I bet she's rich, but they'd need to haul her away to prison instead of getting money from her. Poor prisoners, when she turned up. Poor horses pulling the wagon they'd take her away in, off to jail. She doesn't like horses, either. Anything alive, Mrs. Hopkins doesn't like. She has dolls in her house. Dead dolls with painted-on faces. No husband. She pets her dolls, they say. That's because she's doolally, not right in her nasty old head. Dolls in her front room, leaned up near the window, and extra sausage—she thinks I don't see her, but I do.

Frognal House has high windows. You can see and see. You can see yourself sick and all to blazes with so much light. So much looking can make you dizzy, but you have to. It's your duty. The nurse said to me at the beginning—when we arrived here the first time, me and my mum—she said, "You have to look, please, because that's only fair to them." She was speaking to me, but it felt like she meant for my mum to listen, too, and the three of us were rushing like anything, which seemed odd. We were nearly running down these long corridors that were made of wood, these thin platforms with a roof and no sides, and the rain was clattering overhead and our feet were making hollow noises underneath—*clatter* and *bang*—and my mum was already worried because the wet had spoiled her shoes and she doesn't like it when she's rushed. She didn't want to be out of breath and flustered when she saw my dad. She hates to be flustered and it happens to ladies very easily, so my job as a gentleman is to make things be calm.

I felt a bit sick, though, and couldn't be calm.

And the nurse was pelting along, and we had to follow or we would have gotten lost, because I didn't have the compass yet and couldn't set a direction.

Mum didn't want my dad to see her in spoiled shoes. I remember thinking he'd be used to mud everywhere and not being able to polish his boots and he wouldn't worry. But coming up the road to the hospital, past the blue benches, she'd just kept on: "My shoes are spoiled. My new shoes. I didn't want him to see me in a state."

The shoes and the rain — rattling rain — and the nearly running were making her think she would be in a state. And I wanted to help, and my dad had said I should. He said while he was away that was my job, and him being in the hospital was still him being away and not living with us. So I held my mum's hand. She was upset, and holding hands always makes things better.

I held her hand right through the hospital.

"Promise that you'll keep looking," the nurse kept on, and I promised.

And I did look.

I always look, even at Private Minshull, who's horrible to me and horrible to everyone and says bad words when he thinks my dad can't hear him. Private Minshull caught one at Messines. Dad tells him that he doesn't know anything and never has and that the ink on Minshull's number is still wet and so's he. I don't know what that means, but it makes Minshull laugh. He doesn't have a good laugh.

I think it's our job to look at the men here, because there aren't any mirrors, not anywhere, and so without other people seeing them, the patients might believe they're not really there.

The men have sky-blue uniforms to show they're wounded — blue suits and white shirts and very red ties, like blood and bandages, only not so much like that, because they're not frightening. They don't scare me. Nobody in here scares me. I told my dad that, and it was true. It still is true.

The blue benches outside are for the blue men, as if whatever they touch in the world will turn blue.

Mum said it's so that people know the men might come and sit on the benches and worry them. They are nothing to worry about, though—so that means that people are mainly a thick-headed lot, like my dad said.

Patients get to wear their own caps, so those are all different for each regiment. That way the tops of their heads are still at home the way they should be. My dad has a navy-blue tam-o'-shanter, because that's what a London Scottish man gets. He's from London, but he's a Buchanan and a Scotsman, and he picked the London Scottish Regiment so that he could be both things at once. In his going-away picture, he was wearing his kilt, which is hodden gray—*hodden* is a Scottish type of gray—and not the exact same tam-o'-shanter that belongs to him now. The Germans made him lose his first one, and so the hospital requisitioned him another. His cap badge has a silvery lion on it. It's the Scottish type of lion, standing up and waving its arms at you, so you'll keep away or face the consequences.

Sometimes, when I'm with my dad, I just look at the lion and I read the badge over and over—**LONDON SCOTTISH STRIKE SURE**. It's a brave lion.

Mum is not Scottish; she's London without anything else added. But she must be fond of the Scottish type of people, because she married my dad and she lives with me.

When he was home on leave, she would be careful with his kilt and make it clean and get rid of the little visitors it would bring with it in the folds. She said it was a perishing shame sending our boys home like that.

She likes my dad.

When he went to be in the army, she put his picture in the special frame where the two of them in their wedding clothes used to be, and she dusted it every morning and every night with a cloth she didn't use for anything else, and all of his letters are in a tin that smells of the army and not like him. She reads them sometimes.

She likes my dad.

It's only me that comes to see him, though.

After that time when it rained and her shoes were spoiled, she didn't come back.

When I said he would be sad if she wasn't there, she shouted at me and then hugged me, which didn't make sense.

I think she got scared when she saw Dad was all bandages — except his one eye. You could see his eye, seeing you.

And it was his sad eye. In his going-away picture, if you looked at it proper hard, he had a sharp kind of eye, which was for when he was being funny and giving orders and getting things done, and his other eye seemed more soft, and that would be the one that was in charge when he was singing songs or talking about his mum or saying how green it was in Scotland. Which used to be when my mum would say it was green and ignorant and never washed, and then his sharp eye would spark up and he'd go over and tickle her and say she would rather have a Scotsman than anything and make her hit him a little bit and squeal and send me upstairs, because of him being ridiculous.

His sad eye is the one that he's still got.

Putting your head up over the top to see — Dad says he told his men they couldn't duck down faster than a bullet and they should keep their heads dropped out of sight. And he was careful himself, which showed them how.

But he still caught one.

They say that you catch a bullet or a bit of shrapnel, only you can't catch either of those things — they go right through, so everyone should just shut up about it. My dad got hit by shrapnel. He didn't *catch* anything; he got *hit*.

When my mum saw him and the bandages and how his eye was sad, she just sat down very fast. We were upstairs in his room, only with the other men not there — because they were well enough to be out and about — and she sat on Barnes's bed without knowing it was Barnes's and made the coverlet have ripples in it and held her own hands, one in the other.

I went and tried to hug him, only made sure to be careful in case I hurt him, but he made his arms very tight around me and I could tell he was fine, really. He held me squashed against his shirt, which smelled of the army and something sour, but like him, too. He was like he always had been, except for where the bandages were.

I don't know why my mum didn't understand that.

Maybe she had been understanding other things for a long time and then got tired and had to stop. She seemed tired, the way she dropped down on Barnes's bed. And she didn't say anything for a while.

I told Dad that on Sunday evenings while he was in France, me and Mum would sing the soldiers' songs we knew he liked, and she would say he might be singing them at the same time and that way we were all together. She understood that like it was true. We'd sing, *"We shall want you and miss you but with all our might and main / We shall cheer you, thank you, bless you when you come back again."*

It wasn't the right words to say *bless you*—that was supposed to be *kiss you,* only boys don't kiss their dads, and I had to be able to join in. And I don't know what *main* is—another way of missing him, I think. That bit of the chorus made up for the other, which said that we didn't want to lose him but we thought he ought to go.

It was him who thought he ought to go—married men didn't have to when he volunteered, but he said that everyone would have to be in uniform in the end and he'd get a better place if he went early. That's how he got to start as a private but end up as a two-pip lieutenant—because he stayed in so long and did so much and went to so many places.

We are all tired. I think everybody is tired.

In the end, I got tired, too, and stopped talking while my dad put his arm around me, still tight, and it got very quiet. I could hear the rain on the slates—*clatter, bang*—and the way the wind pushed at the windows in their frames—*clatter, bang*.

Then my dad said, "On you go, son. Ak dum, ak dum, off you run. They'll have a tray of buns downstairs." And he started telling me how to get to the lounge where the officers play their gramophone and have the papers to read and the *Illustrated London News*, with all the scribbly kind of drawings that Dad likes.

Only Mum said, "He can't go down there by himself."

And my dad asked her, "Why not?"

Which she didn't answer. She stood up instead and went to where he was sitting on his bed and started to hit him, not so much, but then more, on his chest, and she was being careful not to hit his head and where he was all bound up, but she was still hitting him hard until he caught her hands.

Then he told me, "You go and find those buns, Frank." And he gave me the directions again and the compass, while Mum was resting her forehead on his chest, not noticing anything.

And I think she was crying, because her shoulders shook like they did when she got the telegram from the army about what happened—the one about Dad—but she wasn't making any noises, so I couldn't tell, not really.

That was when I got the compass.

"You keep ahold of that, and it'll see you right. And then come back here and you can take your mother home, like a good man. If anyone asks, say you're following Lieutenant Buchanan's orders."

I didn't want to go, but I did.

I never found the buns, though. I just sat at the bottom of the stairs, and this man—who was Hepplewhite—came and talked to me about sailing toy boats, which I never have, but he did and enjoyed it when he was small.

Hepplewhite was the first man I saw with a "Fray Bentos" face. That's what he called it. He said in the old days people wouldn't have lived if they got hurt in their faces or heads, but now they did. He said that was a funny thing and laughed, only his mouth is a bit odd, so his laugh was odd, too.

That was the first time I heard a Fray Bentos man laugh.

He said that the hospital people had taken plaster and made a cast of his face and that now the Tin Noses Shop was going to make him a tin piece to fit and he'd wear it and seem just like anyone else. He said they'd do the same for my dad, once they'd made the best of him.

He'd get a glass eye, like they have in dolls. And a bit of his face back, only painted on the tin. But it would look right. He'd even get eyelashes—they make them out of metal, too, in little strips.

Then, after a while, my dad came downstairs with my mum, arm in arm, which is how they went strolling on Sundays, so I thought it was going to be all right.

But Hepplewhite scared her.

And when he laughed, that scared her.

And it wasn't his fault, but I still don't like him for it.

Once my dad gets his new face, though, he says things will be fine. The surgeon made him all fixed up where he was wounded and—after the changes got done—I'm used to how he is, and I've said there's nothing much wrong now and he won't need a mirror, because he can grow a beard like in the navy so he won't need to shave.

And I brought him his going-away picture, because Mum put it in a drawer and won't notice it's gone, and the men and women at the Tin Noses Shop—proper artists—will copy who he used to be. They will make him a mask with another eye, like his clever, happy eye, and he'll wear it held on with glasses, fitted right over the part that got hit. And no one will be able to tell the difference from how he was.

He will be like himself, only better. Everyone will see.

Previous page: **SOLDIER AND SON**
At the time of the First World War, plastic surgery was still quite primitive, so artists at special studios in London and Paris made detailed copper masks for soldiers with serious facial disfigurements. Only a fraction of affected soldiers received masks, as each one took a month to make.

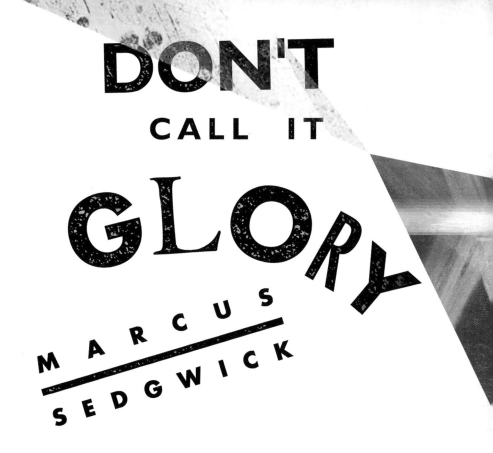

DON'T
CALL IT
GLORY

MARCUS
SEDGWICK

The boy's name does not matter.

Neither does that of the angel, sitting in the tree nearby.

The boy knows only that it is September, that his mother is waiting for him at the end of the street, and that he is late for school.

The angel knows only that something draws him to this place.

The boy's mother calls him again, wearily, and he gets as far as the withered oak outside number 9 before he stops again. She sees him looking at the tree. Then he points.

He says something, but he's too far away for her to hear.

He turns and says it again, louder.

What's that?

She hangs her head.

Dear God, she thinks, *it's a tree. And it's been there all your life.*

What she says is, *Hurry up. We're going to be late. Again.*

Finally he comes, and she drags him around the corner so hard his toes barely touch the ground.

The boy tries to tell his mother about the thing he saw in the tree, but she won't listen again this morning. He shuts up. He'll try on the way home, after school.

The angel watches them go, listening.

For a moment, he thought the boy had seen him, but that would be impossible. Yet the boy *had* seen something, something no one else has seen in many, many years. A shard of dark metal, sunk into the trunk of the tree. The bark has grown around it as the years have passed, almost absorbing the whole thing into its body, but not quite.

There's still the tip of age-dulled steel poking from between the folds of the bark.

The angel slips down from his branch. He winces slightly as he jars his knees on landing, something that makes his thoughts pause for a moment, something that begins to pull him into the past, but then he sees the metal the boy saw, and that takes all his attention. He stands close to the oak, peering at the metal as if sniffing it. He stays that way for a long time. He's still standing like this when there's a voice right beside him.

Look! says the boy. *I told you.*

The boy's mother nods, pleased at least that her son wasn't making things up for once, because there have been times when he claims to have *seen* things.

Come inside now, she tells him. *I have to get your tea on and I have to work tonight and Granddad will be here soon,* and all the boy hears is *and and and . . .*

As they go inside, the angel turns, wondering. *Did I stand there all day,* he thinks, *and not notice?* He doesn't feel like he wants to leave the tree, because he believes that's where his answers lie, but he does, because he wants to follow the boy more.

By the time the angel walks into the kitchen, time has moved again, and the boy's mother has gone out.

The boy is sitting at the table, pushing beans on toast into his mouth without awareness. The TV is on in the next room. His grandfather is sitting across the table from him, smiling at his grandson when he's not drifting off somewhere else. He's seventy-four years old.

Granddad? asks the boy.

The old man opens his eyes. He smiles and asks what the matter is.

Nothing's the matter, says the boy. *I just want to know something. I want to know what that piece of metal is in the tree.*

Metal? asks the old man. *Tree?*

So the boy explains, and when he's done, his grandfather is nodding.

It's not the sort of thing you can find in a history book, is it? he says. And then he tells the boy what he needs to do: that he ought to speak to Mr. Evans at number 43.

The angel walks around behind them both, circling slowly, his eyes wide, as the old man explains to his grandson that, as far as he can remember, Mr. Evans was born on Tempest Avenue. And Mr. Evans is even older than he is. If anyone knows, Mr. Evans will.

The boy does not go and speak to Mr. Evans, not for a month, during which the angel sits in the branch of the tree, and during which time rests. Then, with a single tick of the clock, the month has passed and the boy marches out of his house, determined not to be afraid to speak to the old man at number 43.

He walks fast so he'll get there before he loses his nerve, and the angel scrambles out of the oak after him, landing on his hands and knees in the dry earth under the tree. His thoughts pause. He can almost see something in the ground beneath him.

Then he lifts his head and sees the boy at the open door of

number 43. Old Mr. Evans is there. The boy is going inside. The door is closing.

The angel runs, cursing his slowness.

As he comes into the sitting room, he fears it's too late, that he will have missed what he needs to hear, but he need not have worried. Few people have time for Mr. Evans now. But he knows the boy's mother, and she at least is kind enough to say hello when they pass. And the boy has just asked him a question that has opened his memory, which now gapes wide, flooding the room with recollections.

The angel marvels at Mr. Evans's face. His skin is thin and mottled and folded in deep creases. When he frowns, deep furrows cross his forehead. When he smiles, the lines pile up across his cheeks and under his eyes. The angel has never seen anyone so old.

Yes, Mr. Evans is saying. *I was born here. My mother and father bought the house new. The whole street was new. Took a chunk out of the parkland and turned it into houses, they did. Good houses they built then. That was between the wars. In 1933 it was, and I came right along. To keep them busy.*

He winks and smiles.

The angel smiles, too. He likes Mr. Evans already.

The boy is asking about the tree, about the metal, and then Mr. Evans's, eyes widen a little.

Yes, I can tell you about the metal. Thought it was all gone now. Inside the tree. You've got sharp eyes, son. Sharp eyes. See more than most, do you?

The boy doesn't understand that and so he doesn't know what to say, but it doesn't matter, because Mr. Evans is telling him a story.

Mr. Evans tells him how it was when he was seven years old, or was it eight? The war had begun, so he must have been at least six.

The First World War? asks the boy.

Mr. Evans laughs. *World War Two,* he says. *How old do you think I am?*

The boy has no idea. Neither does the angel.

Mr. Evans goes on with his story. *I was playing with my big brother and our sis and some other kids from the street. We were playing war, up and down Tempest Avenue. It was a hot day! I remember that, and I remember the old woman who came out and shouted at us. Mrs. Bentley, she was.*

Everyone scarpered. Scram! Except me. I just stood there like a dummy, didn't I, while Mrs. Bentley told me off. She said what we were doing was wrong — making a game of it all, she meant. We'd been playing at dogfights, pretending we were in the RAF, shooting down imaginary Luftwaffe, and Mrs. Bentley told me I was a wicked boy, that I should have more respect. I was ter-rified! I just stood there. . . . Oh, I remember one more thing: that it was the first time I saw someone shouting and crying at the same time, and when I went home and told Mother about it, she told me that Mrs. Bentley's husband had been killed in the war. That's the First World War, says Mr. Evans, winking.

He stops, and the boy sits, waiting for more, but there is no more.

The angel stares at Mr. Evans, and feels his mind turning, trying to make sense of it, but the boy is speaking again.

But the tree, he says. *What about the metal in the tree?*

Mr. Evans pulls himself back. He laughs.

Silly me, he says. *Yes, you asked me about the tree.*

And then he explains about the oak, under which Mrs. Bentley was standing as she shouted at him.

When the tree got its name, Tempest Avenue didn't exist, he explains, laughing at how the boy's eyes widen at that idea. He says it again. *When the tree got its name, Tempest Avenue didn't exist. Back then, in the first war, it was all fields around here, and the town itself was no more than a village. The first war; that was the time of the zeppelins. They came in the night, great ghosts, too high to see most of the time. But they dropped bombs, and we could do nothing about it, not till they invented the incendiary bullets. Then we started to fight back! Well, one night, October of 1916, one of our pilots brought down one of their airships, and it crashed, a burning fireball, straddled right across that oak. Talk of the town, they said it was. People came from London to see it: the Zeppelin Oak. Imagine that! They caught trains from London to see the wreck!*

It's a piece of an airship? asks the boy, his eyes wide.

Mr. Evans is nodding.

The angel is clutching for something to lean up against. He staggers to the wall of the sitting room and finds that he is having trouble breathing. His heart pounds as it hasn't done in years, and his thoughts are tumbling out of the room and into the air, and he feels everything collapsing around him as he understands why he sits in the low branch of the oak tree.

That was *his* airship that crashed. He was not the captain; that was Kapitänleutnant Mathy. The angel was the *Steuermann:* the steersman. That was when he died. That was when they all died.

The angel flees as bits and pieces of that night come back to him, but not all of it. Not yet. He leaves the boy behind. The boy who, now that he has his answer—that the metal in the tree came from a crashed zeppelin—is desperate to leave the old man's house.

Before he goes, old Mr. Evans has one last thing to tell him.

You know, he says, remembering, *I saw Mrs. Bentley again. A few days after she shouted at me. She saw me passing her house and called me to her door. Gave me some sweets. Said she was sorry.*

The boy spends the next month hunting. He finds some books on local history in the library. He makes an amazing discovery:

why their street is called Tempest Avenue. His mum always thought it must refer to Shakespeare, and so she is mildly interested when her strange son tells her that the name of the pilot who shot the zeppelin down was Wulfstan Tempest.

Wulfstan became a big hero, says the boy. *They made a statue to him, though he never saw it, because he was killed before they put it up.*

Funny, the boy's mother says, a roasting pan balancing in her hands, halfway to the oven.

What, Mum?

That's a German name. Wulfstan. He was a big British hero for shooting down a German ship. That's ironic.

Ironic, Mum? What's that?

But she's fussing over the cooking again now, and doesn't answer.

The boy pesters a teacher that he likes at school, trying to find out more about the war, and he reads difficult books and complicated web pages, seeing what he can find. What he finds is that he starts to see things in a new way. He begins to *feel* why his mum called the fighter pilot's name *ironic,* though he still doesn't understand what it means. He starts to feel things that he doesn't know the words for. The words would be things like *futile,* and *tragedy,* and *unjustified.* He reads about things most people don't read about. Not the glory of the fighting or the statistics of death, or the tanks, the gas, the trenches, the planes, the airships. He starts to feel differently about the war. Less excited. More sad. He wonders what other people who have felt sad have done about it, and how they have remembered the war.

The angel, meanwhile, is sick. He barely feels alive now. As he lies in the highest branches of the tree, he feels as if he's a whispered word in someone else's dream. He rolls and turns like clouds in a storm, but without force. He is weak; he is nearly gone. And then, one day, as if recovering from a long illness, he suddenly lifts his head as the boy marches past, right underneath the tree.

He's too slow; the boy is gone, hurrying to school, calling after his mother to hurry up.

The angel watches her go by, too, and gingerly climbs down from the tree, branch by branch, stepping lightly onto the soil, and as he does so, he realizes something has changed in him, or rather, something has grown in him. He does not know which came first, but he has a new power, and with it he has a new determination.

He examines his power and wonders what he can do.

He soon finds out: standing on Tempest Avenue, with barely a trace of effort on his part, he has wound time back to 1940.

There is old Mr. Evans. Old Mr. Evans is seven years old. The angel just catches sight of Mr. Evans's brother and sister and the other older kids running away down the street, as Mr. Evans himself waits to be berated by Mrs. Bentley.

The angel watches the scene for a moment, then steps inside Mrs. Bentley's mind. He feels all the pain there. Everything is twisted.

He blinks, and moves forward a few days, and things are calmer in Mrs. Bentley's mind. There is still the sadness, like a glowing core inside her, but there is more sorrow than anger now. She's handing the young Mr. Evans a bag of sweets she'd been hoarding. She's saying she's sorry to have shouted, but she doesn't tell him what she's really thinking, because she knows he's too young to understand.

Why should you remember? she thinks. *Wouldn't it be best if you young people never had to know about such things? Go and play your games, Thomas Evans. Go and play.*

The angel sees Thomas Evans run off to share his sweets and his story with his brother and sister, thinking that he had better not let his mother see the precious lemon drops or she'll want to know how he came by them.

From Edith Bentley's mind, it's a short step into the presence of her husband, Jack. The night the zep comes down on the oak is the night Jack dies in France. Edith's living in the East End of the city. She's had just two letters from her husband. He's been away for six months, and it will take her another two to hear that Jack is dead. He never wanted to sign up. Edith was ashamed. Four times someone pushed a white feather into his hand, and still he refused to go. When they enacted the draft in March 1916, she said one thing to him: *You should have gone before they made you.*

The angel hears those words in Jack Bentley's head as he goes over the top toward the Transloy Ridges. For the 47th Regiment, it's a victory of sorts, but not for Jack, who's killed instantly by a round from a Maxim gun that enters his eye.

Some of Jack Bentley flies toward the angel—and through him—and the angel moves, through time and space again, to a time on the street when a young woman, ignoring Edith, steps up to Jack and puts a feather in his hand, muttering one word at him.

The angel watches Jack's face. And Edith's. And that of the woman, who's just called him *Coward*. The angel slips through all their minds and finds pain in each of them. Finding it too much to take all at once, he retreats to his tree, the oak, once more.

There's the boy again.

He's walking to school. He's alone. He's told his mother he's old enough to go by himself, and he doesn't want to be late. It's a special day today because they're going to be *remembering the war.*

The angel wants to go, too. He slips from his tree and soon catches up with the boy, for though the boy is walking fast, the angel feels lighter than he has felt in a long while.

It's not far to school. They round a corner and head along the upper part of the main street. There's an old man standing outside a shop. He has a cardboard tray suspended by a cord around his neck, and he's selling red paper flowers. As the boy passes him, the old man stares at him for a second, at his chest, and then waves a fist.

For shame! the old man cries, and the boy feels himself shudder in fright.

The angel puts an arm out, around the boy, almost touching him, and glares at the old man who shouted.

The boy lifts his head, but that's as much as he can do, and he hurries on to school. The angel dallies briefly; he flies through the flower seller's mind and learns that he has been in no wars, though he thinks he would like to have been.

The angel feels the anger in the man's mind; it is righteous and unshakable.

Young people! he declares to himself, over and over. *Young people!*

Fascinated by this, the angel finds that he is delayed. The boy has gone, up the street, around the corner, and in through the school gates. The angel hurries after him, feeling his way, and finds the boy on the playground.

The boy's teacher is towering above him. She's shouting. Around them is a small circle of the other children.

Give it to me! demands the teacher.

The boy does not move.

Give it to me!

Now, reluctantly, the boy pulls the poppy he made at home from his sweater and hands it to the teacher. It is white.

Put this one on instead! she barks, and hands him her own poppy.

It is red.

As soon as the teacher is gone, the other children swarm around the boy. The usual bullies are there, the ones who know he is different from them.

What's that supposed to mean?

It's for peace is all he will get to say.

Then they're on him.

First with words.

Peace? says one of the bigger boys. *You'd have been peaceful if the Germans came over here and raped your sister?* The big boy doesn't even know what *raped* means, but he heard his father say it once. *Peace? Wimp! Coward!*

Then come the fists. The angel leaps forward and tries to stop them but finds he can't. He tries to hold them off, but they go right through him. The boy hunches over and waits for it to stop. He tries to stop himself from crying, but he can't. And he can't even explain that he's not crying because they're hitting him but because he doesn't have the words to explain what he means. He can't explain why he wanted to wear a white poppy and not a red one, because it's too hard for him. It's too complicated. Maybe when he's older, he'll be able to express it all, but for now the thoughts in the bigger boys' minds are much simpler and more easily expressed.

The angel doesn't need to go inside their minds to see those thoughts. He's seen them himself. A hundred times. When he was alive. When he was alive, he thought such simple things himself.

With that thought, the angel is tumbling far, far away, through space and through time, and then, here he is. At the helm of the airship L31.

But this is not the night he dies. This is another raid, just a week before. Kapitänleutnant Mathy is in command, as usual. The L31 is one of the first three "super-zeppelins," and Heinrich Mathy, just thirty-three years old, is the darling of the German Naval Airship Division. His men, as on all the other airships, are volunteers. The dangers are many. So high up, the cold can kill, even in summer, when the altitude makes the temperature drop to thirty below. The air is thin, so they suck oxygen from breathing tubes to combat altitude sickness. There is the danger of falling from the narrow ladder that links the gondola to the body of the ship. There is the fact that they have replaced their machine guns with fake ones, which are much lighter, and which might still scare away enemy aircraft. For the same reason—lightness—they have discarded their parachutes, a regular practice, and one that leaves all the men having to ponder, at some time or other, whether, if hit by enemy fire, they would prefer to burn or jump.

The angel is light now. He is glad he gives no extra weight to the airship that was once his, for height is the one sure defense they have against the British planes. He floats next to Heinrich Mathy for a while. He ponders his captain from just behind his shoulder as he speaks into a communication tube over which he can just hear the voice of his bomber.

In a fragment of time so small as to be unseen, the angel goes to sit with the bomber. He listens in on the bomber's thoughts and hears that he is already writing his report in his head. Later, these words will be set on paper, but the angel is treated to a preview.

Visibility was exceptionally good. With perfect clearness, the Thames bridges, the railway stations, even the Bank of England, could be recognized. In less time than it takes to tell, I pushed the levers and anxiously followed the flight of the bombs.

This is what the bomber, a man called Schramm, will write in his report. Only the angel hears some extra thoughts that Schramm has.

These bombs are our greeting to London.

The angel retreats.

He knows that he is aboard the L31 — he could go and see, but he cannot bring himself to do so.

Suddenly the bombs are falling, and the angel drops with them, on impulse.

They rain on Dalston, and a house on Ball's Pond Road is demolished instantly. The explosion sends shrapnel flying across the street. A woman in bed who has been woken raises her head, the top of which is removed by a chunk of flying metal. Next door, the houses are on fire.

The angel stands and watches. He watches for hours as the houses burn, and the efforts of the people to put the fires out are puny and in vain. The airships have long gone, halfway back to the Continent by the time dawn breaks, and more and more people begin to gather outside the ruined houses.

The angel realizes he has lost track of time again when he sees that the morning is half over. A line has formed outside one of the ruined houses. A man is charging people a penny to go inside and see the horrors. The angel joins the back of the line, shuffling along with everyone else, though he has no need of a coin to get inside. Inside, where an elderly couple sit roasted, on their knees, side by side. Their clothes are burned off them. The man's arm is around his wife's waist. They are by the side of their bed. Still praying.

Repulsed, the angel flees and finds himself passing through the streets of London and the minds of the people there.

He's caught by a young woman in a hotel. She's writing a letter home.

It was a most wonderful and thrilling sight! I turned out of bed and saw two zeps right above the city. This is the nearest I have reached to being under fire and very exhilarating it was, too.

He slips in and out of other heads and finds similar feelings, as well as ones of terror.

He finds himself in the head of a young British officer on leave. The man was a poet before the war, one who is starting not to believe in the rightness of it. He describes the zeppelin attack in his diary that evening, but in truth he has seen worse things out in France. Things that will one day make him preach for peace — after, that is, he recovers from a mental breakdown.

The angel passes through him, and on, and finds he needs to see the boy again.

It's hard to pull himself away from the past this time. He is starting to feel heavier again, much heavier, and it takes an enormous effort of will to get into the future once more, but finally he does it.

He finds the boy sitting in his living room on Tempest Avenue. The boy's mother is at the other end of the sofa, half watching the TV, on which the news is showing pictures of a solemn ceremony: earth has been dug up in Belgium and carefully brought to London under armed guard. The soil is in bags piled reverentially on a gun trolley; some of it has been put into a polished oak casket. A thousand soldiers in full ceremonial uniform stand by, saluting the soil in which British and French and Germans died a hundred years ago.

Watching the TV, the angel flashes into the minds of just three of the soldiers who died out there in France in 1916. His passing through their consciousness gives them the understanding of what is being done with the soil, and they piss themselves laughing at the pointlessness of it—though one of them smiles wryly, since it was liquid mud that drowned him, facedown in a shell hole.

The angel snaps back to the living room again.

The TV has been turned off, and the room is dark. Time has passed.

He searches upstairs, but the boy is not in his room. The house is empty. The angel hunts up and down, then staggers out into the street. He runs through the town and up the path to the boy's grandfather's house, where he finds the boy asleep on the sofa. His mother is dozing in an armchair next to her father's bed. The old man is ill.

The angel leans in close to listen to the man's breathing. It's shallow but still strong. The boy's grandfather will be alive for a while yet. Then the angel leans close to the woman. He feels his way carefully into her mind, since he doesn't want to wake her. She's dreaming, and even in her dreams, she worries about her son, about why he has to be different from everyone else. Before he goes, the angel makes a decision, and, stepping into her dreams, he leaves behind a more positive thought in her mind. That maybe her son being different is a good thing. That maybe it's the people who are different who take us all forward, in the end.

That done, the angel drops through the floor, gently, so gently, and goes to sit by the boy.

For a time, he does nothing. He doesn't try to enter the boy's mind. He just sits. And then he sees that there is something in the boy's clenched hand. He recognizes it at once: it's the piece of shrapnel from the oak tree. As soon as he sees it, the angel has a vision of the boy, late one evening, digging at the old bark with a kitchen knife, until finally he gets it free.

The angel's heart begins to hammer in his chest.

He stares at the piece of his airship.

Unable to stop himself, he reaches out a shaking hand, and with one fingertip, he touches the metal.

The moment he does so is the moment he is undone.

Whirling away into the ether, the angel goes spiraling back in time and in space, no longer in control, no longer with any choice of where or when he goes, dragged howling back and back.

As he travels, he flies through the minds of a million people.

He flies through the mind of the prime minister, on the eve of his great speech to the nation to commemorate the war. His speech has been written and rewritten a dozen times. Every word has been carefully weighed, assessed, and after all of that, there's even some of what he wrote himself before his speechwriters took over. He wants to sleep, because tomorrow will be a big day, an important day for the country, or so he tells himself. There is one word on the paper before him, however, that is causing him to worry. Should the word be there or not? The word is *glorious*.

Before the angel sees more, he finds himself in the mind of a writer who is making a story about the war. Or trying to. He wants to write about the war, and he wants to tell the truth, but he has just realized that it cannot be done. For in order for a story to work, it has to have a purpose, a structure, a journey, and a resolution. And in reality, war has none of these things. War is simply a near-random sequence of horrors, and so to make a story out of war is to lie. The writer thinks about a filmmaker who made such a film. A war film that had no logical path, that did not tell a story, that did not resolve itself. It was an honest film, but no one went to watch it. Unable to proceed, the writer stares at his computer screen.

The angel cares not.

The angel has gone, impelled by the touch of the metal of his downed airship to return to the moment of his death.

Wulfstan Tempest has just rolled his plane alongside the zeppelin and emptied an entire cartridge of incendiaries into it.

The ship is now no more than a fireball of gas and metal, heading for the English field.

The next day, they will come. They will come and see the wreck of the airship whose destruction caused a cheer that could be heard from one end of London to the other.

They will pile into trains from the city and walk the two miles through the mud to the field where the zeppelin lies broken over the oak. They will buy pieces of metal as souvenirs from the soldiers guarding the wreck, and when they run out, the soldiers will sell any old piece of metal they can, passing each one off as the real thing.

Only the angel knows the difference, because as he materializes on the falling airship and becomes one with his living self for the first time in a hundred years, he knows he will remain connected to the metal of his ship, and the place it falls, forever.

He considers whether he should burn or jump.

He remembers the boy. The boy in the future. The boy who could see a little bit more than the others, who saw the shrapnel in the oak, and freed him.

He remembers the first time he jumped from the tree and jarred his knees, and how, when he fell on his hands and knees the second time, he thought he could see something in the ground.

He knows what that thing is now.

It is the impression of a body, six inches deep in the hard ground, a body with arms out wide and legs splayed.

He knows the answer to his question: Burn or jump?

The angel jumps, and as he realizes what he is doing, he realizes something else. He is no angel. He does not have wings.

Having no wings, he falls to the ground, wheeling through the night sky with the fire of the ship above him like a sun fallen from the heavens.

Having no wings, he falls.

He is not an angel, but a ghost. Nothing more. He's been attached to this spot for a hundred years, waiting for an answer that will not come, because there are no answers, only questions.

But as he falls, there is one thing he does know, and it's this:

Remember it if you will, and if you will, remember it how you want.

But don't call it glory.

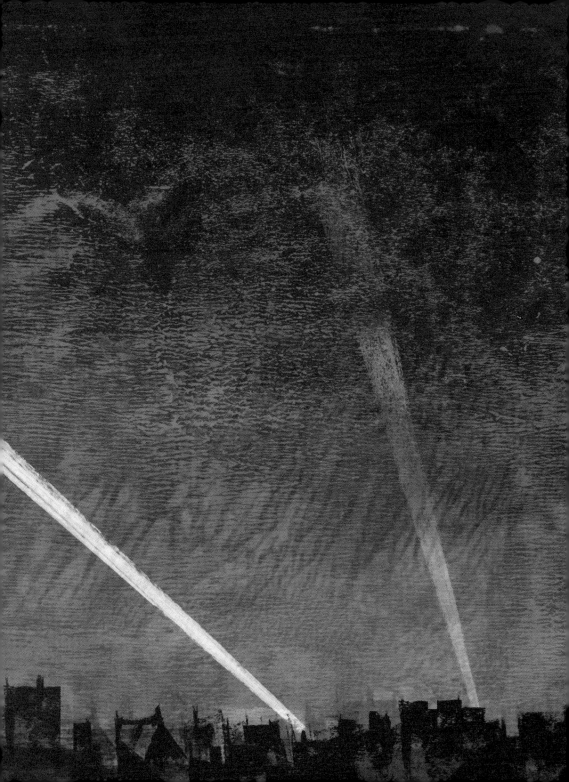

Previous page: **ZEPPELIN RAID**
In 1915, Germany launched a series of bombing raids on
Britain from rigid airships that came to be known as zeppelins,
named for the German manufacturer Count Ferdinand von
Zeppelin. From 1915 to 1918, Germany carried out more than
fifty zeppelin raids on Britain, killing 557 people and injuring
a further 1,358.

THE COUNTRY called HOME

JOHN BOYNE

The brick crashed through the front window shortly after midnight, and Émile woke with a start, his heart pounding, his eyes raw from interrupted sleep. The room was dark, and as he reached across for the wristwatch that lay on the bedside table, he knocked it off and heard it land on the wooden floor with a heartbreaking crack.

"No!" he whispered to himself in dismay.

His father had given him the wristwatch two weeks earlier as a present for his ninth birthday, and he treasured it. Looking down now, he saw that the glass that covered its face had shattered, scattering splinters across the floor. The watch wasn't new, of course. It had belonged to his grandfather, William Cross, who had bought it more than fifty years before on the morning he left Newcastle to begin a new life in West Cork. He'd passed it down to his son, Stephen, who in turn had given it to Émile, telling him that he needed to take great care of it, for it was a precious family heirloom.

And now it was broken.

The boy put his head in his hands, wondering how he would ever tell his dad.

A moment later, he heard his parents' bedroom door open and the sound of their feet running along the hallway into the front parlor of their small cottage, and Émile remembered the noise that had woken him in the first place.

He jumped out of bed, his left foot landing on one of the small shards of glass, and sank to the floor, curling his foot around to examine the damage. A small chip, like a piece of broken ice, was half submerged in the ball of his foot, and he turned his thumb and index finger into a pair of pincers to pull it out, saying one of those words he wasn't supposed to say as it emerged. A spot of blood appeared in its wake, but he pressed his hand against it, and when he took it away again, the blood had disappeared. Standing up, he tested his weight on the injured foot before opening his bedroom door and following his parents into the parlor.

"Émile," said his mother, turning around when she heard him, "what are you doing up?"

His mother, Marie, was wearing her nightgown, and her hair hung down loosely around her shoulders. He hated seeing her like this. She usually wore her hair up in a tight bun, and even though she didn't own many clothes, she always made an effort to look elegant. Stephen, Émile's father, put it down to her French upbringing. He said women looked after themselves over there, not like Irish women, who'd go around in a potato sack every day except Sunday if they could. But like this, in the middle of the night, she looked old and tired and not like herself at all.

"I heard a noise," he said. "It woke me up."

"Don't come over here in your bare feet, son," said Stephen, who had taken yesterday's newspaper off the table and was using a brush to sweep the broken glass from the window onto the front page. Émile could read the headline—*Lusitania Sunk!*—which ran in big letters above a photograph of a four-funneled ocean liner. Everyone in town had been talking about this for days, and prayers had been said in the church for the souls of those who had drowned.

"The window!" said Émile, pointing across the room. A breeze was blowing through, making the lace curtains on either side dance in the early-morning air, like a pair of young girls waltzing in their nightgowns. "What happened?"

"Someone put a brick through it," said Stephen.

"But why?"

"Émile, step back," said Marie, putting her hands on his shoulders and pulling him away from the fragments of glass. "Just until your father is finished."

"Why would someone put a brick through our window?" asked Émile, looking up at her.

"It was an accident," said Stephen.

"How can a brick fly through a window by accident?"

"Émile, go back to bed," said Marie, raising her voice now. "Stephen, should I look outside to see if they're still there?"

"No, I'll do it."

He folded the newspaper into a neat package, the broken glass wrapped carefully inside, and placed it on top of the table before reaching for the latch on the front door.

"Wait," cried Marie, running into the kitchen; she returned with the heavy copper saucepan that she used to make soup.

"What's this for?" asked Stephen, staring at it with a confused smile on his face, the kind of smile he always wore when Marie did something that both baffled and amused him.

"To hit him with," said Marie.

"To hit who with?"

"Whoever threw the brick."

Émile looked around the floor and saw a rectangular shape lying beneath the table, brick-like for certain, but it was enclosed in paper, and the whole parcel was held together by string, like a Christmas present. His mind raced with possibilities of who might have done such a thing. He was currently engaged in a war with Donal Higgins, who lived three doors down, and their acts of retaliation had grown over the last few days. But it was hard to imagine Donal doing something as bad as this, and anyway, he was probably in bed, since he had to go to sleep at eight o'clock every night, while Émile was allowed to stay up until half past.

"I don't think whoever it was will be waiting outside for me, do you?" asked Stephen, opening the front door while Marie stood behind him, holding the saucepan up as he stepped out onto the street. Émile picked up the brick and began to untie the twine. It came loose easily enough, and as the paper unfurled, he was surprised to realize that he recognized it. He smoothed out the creases, pressing it flat against the kitchen table, and examined it carefully. Green, white, and orange, the colors of the tricolor itself, the poster bore a picture of a serious-looking man sporting a big white mustache. The words **TYNESIDE IRISH BATTALION** were written across the top with **IRISHMEN—TO ARMS** inscribed beneath a harp in the center of a shamrock. **JOIN TODAY** was its closing demand.

"What's that?" asked Marie, coming back into the parlor, and Émile lifted the poster to show her, watching as his mother closed her eyes for a moment and sighed before shaking her head, as if she was both surprised and not surprised by what she saw. "I knew something like this would happen," she said. "I said so, didn't I? But your father had to have his own way."

"But why would someone wrap it around a brick?"

"Émile, your foot!" she cried, ignoring the poster now as she looked down at the floor, where a small streak of blood had stained the woodwork. "I told you to keep away from the glass."

But when she sat him down to clean the wound, she was surprised to find no glass there.

"There's no one outside," said Stephen as he came back inside, closing the front door behind him and putting the latch on.

"I knew those posters would only bring trouble," said Marie.

"I know, love, but—"

"Don't *love* me," she snapped—a rare moment of anger, for most days Marie and Stephen seemed to do nothing but laugh together.

"How was I to know they'd attack our house?"

"What did you think they'd do, throw a party for you?"

"I didn't hurt my foot in here," said Émile, unable to meet his father's eyes as he told them what had happened when he woke up. "I'm sorry," he said when he was finished. "It was an accident."

"Ah, Émile," said Stephen, coming over and lifting the boy up to carry him back to bed. "Don't be worrying about something like that. I can fix it. Sure, I've broken the glass many times myself. Trust me, we have bigger things to worry about right now."

Émile had heard the stories many times, but he never grew tired of them:

The story of how his grandfather had left England when all his friends were signing up to fight the Boers in South Africa but he wanted no part of killing people whose names he couldn't even spell correctly. Instead, he came to the south coast of Ireland, where he met an Irish girl, married her, and brought up their son, Stephen, to love dogs, the ukulele, and the novels of Sir Walter Scott.

The story of how Marie left France for Ireland when her parents died and Stephen found her sitting in a tea shop on the afternoon of her twenty-third birthday while he was strolling back to his father's farm.

The story of how he'd sat by the village pump until she came out and he asked her to come to a dance with him some night and she said, *I don't go dancing with strange men,* and he said, *Sure, I'm not strange. Do I seem strange to you? I'm not a bit strange, am I?*

The story of how the dance had gone well, not to mention the wedding at the Clonakilty parish church later that same year, and how they'd wanted a child for a long time but none would come, and only when they'd given up on the idea of it did Émile suddenly appear, out of the blue, a gift to the pair of them, and then their family was complete and neither of them had ever been so happy in all their lives as when there was just the three of them together at home, cuddled up on the sofa, reading their books.

These were stories that Émile had heard many, many times. But sure, how could he ever grow tired of hearing them when they made him feel so wanted, so happy, and so loved?

The posters had arrived four days before the night of the broken window in a long tube sealed in cardboard and brown tape, with eight stamps on the surface bearing the image of King George, who looked like an awful grump. Mr. Devlin, the local postman, waited until evening time to deliver it. Émile suspected that he'd been watching for Stephen to return home from work, and only then did he knock on the door.

"What do you suppose it is?" asked Stephen as he, Marie, Mr. Devlin, and Émile stood at all four corners of the kitchen table, staring at the tube as if it were an unexploded bomb.

"There's only one way to find out," said Mr. Devlin. "Would you not open it, Stephen, no?"

"Ah, I don't know about that," said Stephen, shaking his head and frowning. "Sure, you'd never know what might be in there."

"Oh, for pity's sake," said Marie, taking the bread knife

from the counter and picking up the tube to slice her way down the tape. "We can't just stare at it all night."

"Be careful there, missus," said Mr. Devlin, standing back as if he were afraid that it might blow up in all their faces.

"Will Mrs. Devlin not have your tea on?" she replied, taking the cap off the tube and giving it a shake until the rolled-up sheets of paper eased their way out into her hand. "Should you not be getting home?"

"The food is always burned to a crisp as it is. A few extra minutes won't make it any less edible."

Marie sighed as she held the posters out for everyone to see.

"What's this, now?" asked Mr. Devlin, leaning forward and reading them for himself. "This is something to do with the war, is it?"

Stephen picked up the tube and shook it again, and a note fell out. His eyes moved back and forth across the lines, his lips mouthing the words quietly to himself.

"Good night, Mr. Devlin," he said a moment later, turning to the postman.

"There was something else in there, was there?" he asked, pointing at the note. "Is it an explanation of some sort?"

"Good night, Mr. Devlin," repeated Stephen, opening the front door and standing there with his hand on the latch until the postman gave in and made his way toward it.

"There was a time when a man got a cup of tea when he

visited a house," he announced in an insulted tone as he left. "Those days are gone now, it seems. Good night, all!"

"What's in the note?" asked Émile when there were just the three of them left.

"Maybe you should go to your room," said Stephen.

"Who is it from?" asked Marie.

"James."

"James who?"

"James, my cousin James."

"In Newcastle?"

"Yes."

"And what does he say?"

Stephen cleared his throat and began to read:

"Dear Stephen,

I'm sorry I haven't written in so long, but I'm not a man for letters, as you know. All is well here, but it's raining today. Here are posters that you can post around your town, as we need as many soldiers as we can find or we're going to lose this war. I know all you Irish don't know which side to stand on, but you'll be better off on ours. We'll see you right for it in the end, I'm sure of that.

I have bad news: Do you remember the Williams twins who you used to pal around with when your dad brought you over to see us when you were a lad? Both killed at

Verdun. And Georgie Summerfield, who lived next door to
us? Well, he's been in hospital these last few months; they
say he can't stop shaking or hold a sensible conversation.
It's a rotten business, but — "

Stephen stopped reading and put the letter down.

"Oh," said Marie, her forehead wrinkling a little as she thought about this.

Émile wondered why Georgie Summerfield couldn't stop shaking but guessed it had something to do with the war. It had been going on for almost three years now, since July 1914. His parents and his teachers never grew tired of talking about it, even though it was happening across the sea in Europe, which was *miles* away from West Cork. A boy he knew, Séamus Kilduff, had an older brother who'd signed up to fight with the Brits, and half the town said he was a traitor for taking sides with the English, who'd been making life hell for the Irish for years. The other half said he was very brave to put himself in danger for people he didn't even know and that the only way to secure peace was for everyone who believed in the freedom of nations to do their bit. There was a fierce debate over it, and everyone took a side. Émile heard stories about fights in the local pub and a rule being made on the Gaelic football team that no one could discuss Séamus Kilduff's brother before a game, as it only led to trouble. But then word came that he'd been killed in the Battle of the Somme, and the whole town turned out for his funeral. Father Macallie said he was a credit to his family, a credit to his religion, and above all a credit to West Cork, which would one day achieve independence from the rest of Ireland and be allowed to manage its own affairs as God intended.

A copy of the *Skibbereen Eagle* appeared in their cottage most evenings, and Marie pored over it, engrossed by every piece of information that she could find. Her own country, after all, was being overwhelmed by fighting. Her two brothers had fought to keep the Germans out of their hometown of Reims, but both had been arrested, and she hadn't heard from them in a long time. Émile had learned not to mention their names, as she would only start crying inconsolably.

But Marie wasn't the only one who read the papers. Émile did, too. He'd become interested the previous Easter, when all the trouble had been happening up in Dublin and a group of men had barricaded themselves into the General Post Office on O'Connell Street, demanding that the Irish be left alone to look after Ireland, and the English had come along and said, *Sorry about that, lads, but no chance.* And there'd been lots of shooting and lots of killing, and one of the men from the GPO had been brought out in a terrible sickness, barely knowing who he was or what he was doing, and was tied to a chair so the English could turn their guns on him for showing cheek to their king.

"Why would they fight for the English?" he asked now, looking down at the letter on the table.

"They?" asked Stephen, turning his head quickly and staring at his son; it wasn't often that he had a flash of anger like this. "Who's this *they* that you're talking about, son?"

"The Irish," said Émile quietly.

"The Irish are a *they*, are they?" he asked.

"Stephen, stop it," said Marie.

"Stop what?"

"Just stop it."

"Well, come on, now," said Stephen irritably, shaking his head. "I'll not be having *they*s in this house."

Émile looked from his father to his mother and back again, angry and upset at being spoken to like this. "Well, I don't know, do I?" he cried, trying to hold back tears. "You're English, Mum's French, sometimes you tell me I'm Irish, other times you tell me I'm half-English and half-French."

"You're Irish," said Stephen. "And don't you forget it."

But he wasn't fully Irish; he knew that. The boys at school picked on him and said he was only a blow-in and that if your family hadn't lived in Ireland since before Cromwell had started his slaughter of the innocents, then you had no business being here anyway. And why did he have to be anything? he wondered. The Irish hated the English, the English hated the Germans, the Germans hated the French, so it seemed that if you lived in a country, you had to have someone to hate. But then the Cork people hated the Kerry people, and the Kerry people hated the Dubliners, and the Dubs were split in two, with the families who lived in the tenements in the city center hated by all. It seemed to Émile that you weren't allowed to be alive unless you had someone to hate and someone to hate you in return.

Stephen reached forward and pulled Émile's head into his shoulder for a moment. "I'm sorry, son. I shouldn't have snapped."

Marie stood up, gathering up the posters and taking them toward the fireplace.

"What are you doing?" asked Stephen, staring at her.

"The sensible thing," she said, peeling one off, folding it in half and then half again, before reaching its corner into the flames and letting the fire catch it before she allowed it to sink into the hearth and burn. Then she unpeeled the second one and started to fold it, too, but Stephen was too quick for her; he was on his feet in a jiffy, pulling the posters out of her arms.

"Stop that now!" he shouted.

"Why?"

"They're not for burning."

Émile reached over for the letter, wanting to know what else it said, but Marie pulled it out of his hands and put it on the top shelf of the dresser, next to the key for the outhouse.

"Did no one ever tell you not to read other people's letters?" she asked, staring down at her son.

Émile said nothing in reply but looked at his father instead. "What does James want you to do with those posters?" he asked.

"Post them up around the town. See if any of the men here will sign up."

"Do you think they will?"

Stephen shook his head. "Probably not," he said.

"Then there's no point doing it," said Marie.

"Oh, I'll do it, all right."

"Why?"

"Because it's the right thing."

"The right thing for who?"

Stephen shrugged. "If the Germans win," he said, "if they conquer England, where do you think they'll go next? Think about it, love. What's the next country along?"

Marie threw her arms in the air. "If you put those posters up around here," she said, "our neighbors will call you a traitor. Like they did with Séamus Kilduff's brother."

"Who everyone said was a hero in the end."

"They said he was a hero when they were putting him in the ground. They didn't say anything like that when he walking above it."

"You're not going away to fight, are you, Dad?" asked Émile, his eyes opening wide in horror at the idea.

"I don't know, son," replied Stephen. "But it's something that I've been thinking about. After all, the sooner the war is over, the sooner we can all live in peace."

"No!" shouted Émile, jumping up. "No, you can't. Mum, tell him he can't."

"Stephen, you're upsetting the boy. And throw those things away before they get us all in trouble."

"It's only a few posters. Those who want to take an interest can and those who don't, well, they don't have to."

"Don't be so naive," snapped Marie as Émile rushed to her side and pressed himself against her. "You have no idea what will happen to you if you put them up around town. To us. To all of us. *Irishmen — To Arms,*" she added, laughing bitterly. "They want us on their side when they need help, that's for sure. But when they don't—"

"Us! Them! You! Me!" shouted Stephen. "If you ask me, we all choose our pronouns depending on what suits us at the time!"

And that was the end of that. Marie stormed off to her bedroom, Stephen stayed in the front parlor for a smoke, and Émile grabbed the key for the outhouse and ran down in the cold night air. He'd been desperate to pee ever since Mr. Devlin had arrived with the post, but he couldn't leave the front parlor when there was so much going on.

Émile went with his father when he placed the posters in prominent positions around town, and when the townspeople saw them, there was an outcry. A meeting was held in the church, and Émile listened as Stephen made the case that here was something bigger than the argument between England and Ireland—that, he said, could be returned to at a later date and hopefully with wiser, more peaceful heads—but in the meantime, there was a bigger fight being played out across Europe and the Irish couldn't stick their heads under their blankets forever because sooner or later it would come their way. "We've spent centuries trying to win the land back for ourselves," he told them. "And we're this close. You can feel it. I can feel it. We're on the cusp, lads. Now, tell me, all of you, what if we win our country back and lose it all over again to someone else? Where's the victory in that?"

Donal Higgins's father fought the opposite case. "The enemy of my enemy is my friend," he said. "Did you never hear that line, no? Why on earth would we spend all this time trying to get the English out of Ireland only to help them in their hour of need? Could someone please explain that to me, for it makes no sense as far as I can see!"

"But look, if we help out now, maybe that'll be the difference between victory and defeat," argued Stephen.

"Let them be defeated!" cried Donal Higgins's father.

"And then what? If this war doesn't end soon and with fairness on all sides, you can mark my words that there will be another before too long, and you'll be too old to fight in it, and

I'll be too old to fight in it, but our sons won't! Your Donal will be of age! And my Émile! So think again before you say we should just ignore what's going on."

There was an almighty debate, and Émile couldn't hear any of the arguments anymore as voices were raised so high, and finally Father Macallie had to take to the altar and call the meeting to an end, for it was clear that there was never going to be agreement between the sides, and if it didn't stop, there'd be a fistfight in the church.

Émile sat at the back of the hall and tried to reason it through. He could see both sides. But brave young soldiers were fighting on the Continent to make sure that everyone got to live as they wanted to live. It seemed to him that this was the side worth fighting for.

When he thought about it for too long, however, it made his head hurt; that was the truth of it.

But the posters went up, and Stephen's part in that couldn't be denied. And a few nights later, the brick came flying through the front window, waking up the house and causing Émile to reach out so quickly that his grandfather's watch smashed on the floor.

Six weeks later, when Émile found out that Stephen had signed up to fight for the British Expeditionary Force, he felt frightened and proud at the same time. But he knew that the whole town was in a quandary over it because everyone liked Stephen. He'd grown up among them, after all. He'd married a woman they all respected, had a son who was a fine fellow altogether, and had never done a moment's harm to anyone in his life. Yes, the English were the enemy, but at least they all knew who the English were. If the Germans won, then it was anyone's guess what might happen to Ireland next.

Émile ended up in another fight with Donal Higgins, whose father said that Stephen was a turncoat and a blaggard for falling in with a bunch of English ne'er-do-wells, and if he was any sort of Irishman, then he'd never fight for a country that had done all they could to keep the Irish in servitude for eight hundred years.

"Your dad's a traitor," said Donal Higgins, keeping his left arm close to his waist, his fist clenched, as his right jabbed out and made contact with Émile's chin.

"And your dad's a coward," said Émile, punching low to Donal's waist with his right hand while his left gave him an almighty clatter around the head.

"You take that back," said Donal, kicking out.

"I'll do no such thing," said Émile, launching himself forward and throwing himself on top of Donal, his whole body lashing out in the hope that he'd hit something important and the fight would come to an end as quickly as possible.

It took two teachers to separate them, and they were both given detention for fighting.

They all came out to see Émile off the morning he left for the war, and those who were old enough remembered the day, over twenty years before, when they'd done the same thing for his father. The arguments about the Irish taking part hadn't changed during that time, but no one wanted to see any harm come to one of the town's favorite sons.

He woke early, just after five o'clock, ready to join a small group of young men who were taking a bus together to Rosslare and then a boat across to Plymouth and a train to the center of England, where they were to be taken to a camp to begin basic training. Lying in bed, his eyes on the ceiling, he wondered whether he would survive whatever was to follow and whether he would ever see West Cork again. Whether he would ever again hold his wife in his arms or take a hurley stick out to the fields with his son as he'd done every Saturday morning for the last few years. And finally, the minutes passed, and what choice did he have but to get out of bed, wash, dress in the uniform they'd given him, and get himself ready to say his good-byes?

They gathered on the street, his wife crying for fear of what might happen to him, his nine-year-old son standing in the corner of the doorway, trying his best to be a brave man, even though every part of him knew that he might never see his father again.

"I'll write when I get there," said Émile.

"Make sure you do," she said.

"You're the man of the house now," Émile said, turning to the boy. "You look after your mother while I'm gone, do you hear me, Stephen?"

"I will, Dad," said Stephen, standing up tall, determined not to cry while the whole street was watching him.

"Now, take this," said Émile, reaching into his pocket and handing over his grandfather's watch, whose glass had been broken and mended half a dozen times over the years but still told the time without fail. "It's a family heirloom. And you look after it for me until I get home, all right? Because I'm coming back here for that watch and for you."

They drove across to Rosslare in silence for the most part. Donal Higgins told a few jokes, and the others tried to join in, but the truth was they were too afraid of what was to come to join in the laughter. Émile sat, staring out the window, thinking of his father and all that he'd suffered during the last war, the one they called the Great War. He'd put up those posters, he'd tried to recruit people to fight for what was right, and the people of the town had turned on him, but he had fought on regardless and finally taken four of the lads from the town with him to the trenches, where all but one of them had fallen, all but one of them had given their lives for peace, all but one of them were buried in a cemetery where their families could only visit once or twice in their lives, for wasn't the price of the boat across to the Continent just shocking?

Stephen hadn't been the one to come home. He'd died just short of a year after arriving in France. He'd written home every week while he was there, and he'd kept his spirits up and stayed good-hearted, and he'd been sure that whatever the differences were between England and Ireland, the war was something bigger than all of that and every good man needed to play his part for peace.

And now it was his son's turn.

Émile met his sergeant, he trained, he collapsed in exhaustion, and then he got up again. He felt his body grow thick with muscle, he thought he could give nothing more, he had no more to give, and then he gave some more. He collapsed under the pain of it; he fought out the other side of it. He realized that he was made of strong stuff, that he was his father's son. He reached the end, he passed out, he was applauded, and he took another train to Southampton, where he boarded a boat for France and the uncertainty that lay ahead.

He lay in his bunk the night before the first battle began and thought of that night when he was just a boy and a brick had come through the parlor window and life as he knew it began to change.

"What's your name?" asked the young man in the bed next to his.

"Émile," said Émile.

"You're French?"

"My mother is. My father was English. He died in the Great War."

"And where are you from?"

Émile hesitated. It still came down to this, didn't it? Who you were, where you came from, how you defined yourself. The country you called home.

"I'm Irish," he said, before rolling over and trying to get some sleep.

Previous page: **THE LUSITANIA**
In 1915, the RMS *Lusitania*, a British ocean liner, was sunk by
a German U-boat twelve miles off the coast of Ireland, killing
1,196 people, 124 of whom were American. The incident
strongly influenced the United States' decision to enter the
war in 1917.

WHEN THEY WERE NEEDED MOST

TRACY CHEVALIER

When Jack banged the front door shut, three things told him his mother wasn't home. First, she didn't shout at him for slamming the door so hard. Second, there was no fire lit, and it was freezing. Third, there were no good smells to greet him. No bangers and mash, no fish and chips, not even toast.

She was working late. Again. He and Molly would have to go next door to eat with the Wilkinsons, an elderly couple who always had a runny egg and boiled cabbage for tea. The Wilkinsons had seven hens, named after Snow White's dwarves, and eggs were often on the menu.

"Don't be selfish," his mum had snapped when he'd complained yesterday. "I'm helping out so soldiers like your dad can have Christmas presents. With all they're going through, surely you can sacrifice your mum's cooking for a few days."

That had shut Jack up. He didn't tell her that it wasn't the Wilkinsons' cooking so much as the empty house that bothered him. Even though most of the time she was nagging him to do his homework or clean out the fireplace or bring in the coal, he still preferred to know his mum was there, humming at the sink or rummaging through a cupboard or chatting with the neighbors out back. An empty house made Jack feel left out, as if there was something far more exciting going on elsewhere that he didn't know about and hadn't been invited to.

Jack lit a lamp, then cleared the ash from the fireplace. He was just laying the fire when Molly arrived, her satchel heavy with books. Though three years younger, his sister read far more than he did. Too much, his mother complained, because they kept having to buy Molly new glasses. She stood in the middle of the room and gazed at him, the thick lenses magnifying her eyes so that she looked even more serious. He would never have admitted it to anyone, but he was relieved that she had come home now so that he wasn't alone.

"Mum's out," he announced before she could say anything—though Molly usually said little anyway. "We'll have to go to the Wilkinsons'."

Molly put down her satchel. She didn't take off her coat, though—like Jack, she would wait until the sitting room warmed up. Sometimes their coats stayed on all evening. She put her hands in her pockets and stared at him with her over-size eyes.

"You're going to do something bad today," she said.

Jack dropped the match, and it went out. "Damn!"

He glanced over his shoulder as if expecting to hear his mother shout from the kitchen, *Language, Jack!* Luckily Molly was not a tattletale.

"What do you mean, bad? Like swearing?" he asked.

Molly didn't answer.

"Did Clara tell you this?"

"Yes." Molly lifted her chin a little, as if to prepare herself for her brother's scorn.

Jack smirked. He had named Molly's imaginary friend after "clairvoyant." Molly had never corrected him, and the name stuck. "When are you going to kill her off, do you think? Eight's a bit old for an imaginary friend."

Molly sat in one of the chairs by the fire, unbuckled her satchel, dug around, and pulled out a book.

"What exactly am I going to do that's so bad, then?"

"What do you care, since you don't believe what Clara tells me?"

Jack struck another match and held it to the twists of paper they used to start fires. This time it caught, and he sat back on his heels to watch the flames creep from one twist to another, snagging on kindling and eventually reaching the coal. In half an hour, there would be heat. He glanced out the window; they were only just home from school, yet already it was dark. Jack hated December, since there was no time to play soccer outside before night came. It was dark and cold, and only Christmas cheered up the month. But this Christmas there would be little to celebrate. This Christmas there was a war, and his father was fighting in it.

He glanced at Molly, curled up in the chair, head bent over her book, hair hiding her face. The combination of her serious eyes and her certainty always got to him. Besides, sometimes she was right. She always seemed to know when he was about to get into trouble. "What was it Clara told you I would do?"

"She didn't say."

"Come on, Molly. Tell me."

But Molly did not look up from her book, not even when Jack threatened to tickle her, pinch her, or burn the paper dolls she had made the day before. She was good at ignoring him when she wanted to, and left him to stew over Clara's prediction.

After a dour meal with the Wilkinsons—only enlivened by Molly drawing a lion in egg yolk on her plate—Jack was pleased to find his friend Robbie hopping up and down on the doorstep when they got home.

"Look—crumpets!" Robbie cried, holding up a bag. "Got them from the baker—day old. Come on—I've been waiting ages while you've been eating. It's cold enough to freeze the tail off a brass monkey!"

Robbie was rough around the edges—that's how Jack's mum described him—but he had a solid heart. Everyone called him Robbie the Rascal. Jack knew he was more likely to have stolen the crumpets than been given them, but that didn't stop him from toasting one over the fire, smothering it with butter and black-currant jam, and devouring it.

They were toasting a second round when Jack's mother finally arrived home. "All right, then, pets?" she called out as she came through the door. "Hello, Robbie. Your mum well?"

"She is, Mrs. Park, but we've no coal, so I've come here for toasting."

Mrs. Park removed her hat, gloves, scarf, and coat, and changed her boots for slippers. "Put the kettle on, Molly. Jack, have you done your homework?"

"Most of it." Jack had not even started it.

"Well, finish it off. Robbie, you can help him. I assume you've done yours or you wouldn't be here."

Robbie was a better liar than Jack. "Sure, Mrs. P.—I'll just set him in the right direction."

They puzzled over math for half an hour while Molly read and Jack's mother made herself cheese on toast and tidied up the kitchen. With her bustle, she made the house home again. At last she came and sat in one of the chairs by the fire, her bag on her lap. "All right, now, I've brought something to show you."

"What's that, Mum?" Jack hoped she'd brought home something sweet. The Wilkinsons did not do desserts. Crumpets had whetted his appetite for something more.

"You know I've been working flat out this past week, packing those Christmas tins for the men at the front," Mrs. Park explained. "Well, I've brought one home for you. Not to keep, mind," she added. "Just to look at. No touching. I asked the man in charge, and he said it was all right as long as I bring it right back tomorrow." She pulled from her bag a rectangular package wrapped in brown paper, which she began to carefully undo. Jack and Robbie and Molly gathered at her side.

They had first heard about the tins two months before, when it was announced that the young Princess Mary wanted to give a Christmas present to all the men fighting in the war. A collection had begun, and everyone Jack knew had donated something to the fund, even if it was just a penny or two.

Now the gifts were being assembled at the army depot in Deptford. It was no small task to pack half a million tins, and Mrs. Park had volunteered, along with dozens of women in the area, to help out.

The tin was made of brass and about the size of Mrs. Park's hand. Embossed on the lid was a silhouette of Princess Mary surrounded by laurel wreaths and her initials, *M. M.* Around the edges were designs of swords and flags and battleships on rolling waves.

"Christmas 1914," Molly read. *"Imperium Britannicum."*

It was such a beautiful, intriguing object that Jack couldn't help himself: he reached over and ran his finger over the lid.

"Jack," his mum warned, but she didn't stop him. Despite handling hundreds of them a day, she still understood how precious and touchable the tins were.

"Will Dad get one of these?" Jack asked.

"Yes."

They were silent then, thinking of Mr. Park. His letters home were cheerful, but Jack sensed in them things not being said about what he had seen and done. After reading them, his mother often disappeared into the back garden "for some air," she said, and came back with red eyes.

"What's in it, Mrs. Park?" Robbie asked.

Jack's mum prised open the tin and removed a small envelope, which she set on the table. Underneath, side by side and snug in the space, were two bright-yellow packets: one of cigarettes, one of loose tobacco, both stamped with *Her Royal Highness the Princess Mary's Christmas Fund 1914.*

"But Dad doesn't smoke," Jack said.

"There are special tins with chocolate for those who don't smoke. And look, there's this as well." From the bottom of the tin, Mrs. Park took out a brass cartridge case. Pulling out the "bullet" end, she held up a pencil. "That's sterling silver, that is," she said, touching the stub end with its bullet shape. She handed the pencil to Robbie, her admonishment not to touch anything forgotten in the excitement of looking over the goods.

Molly picked up the envelope, opened it, and pulled out a small card. A photo fell out. "Princess Mary looks so grown up with her hair done like that," she said, studying the picture. Then she read aloud from the card: "*With Best Wishes for a Happy Christmas and a Victorious New Year, from the Princess Mary and Friends at Home.*"

They each took turns handling the items. There was something about the cigarette and tobacco packets, the pencil, the card, and especially the tin that made Jack want to hold them. The tin felt solid, heavy, and cold. It was a thing of substance. How strange to think that this very tin would soon be in the hands of a soldier at the front. Maybe even his dad. Though Jack knew that was unlikely—how could one particular tin out of 500,000 get to his father? And shouldn't his dad get chocolate rather than tobacco? But still he wondered. For a moment he felt closer to his dad than any of Mr. Park's letters home had made him feel.

Robbie and Molly seemed equally fascinated—Robbie with

the cigarettes, Molly with the pencil. For once, Jack's mum indulged them and let them take their time. Now they had something new to distract them from the weak fire and their half-empty stomachs.

"All right, now, that's enough," she said at last. "I'll show you how I pack them. You put the pencil in the bottom of the tin. Then the yellow packets side by side. Then put the photo in the card and the card in the envelope—that part's a bit tricky—and pop the whole thing on top. Then shut the lid, and you're on to the next one."

Just then, there was a call from out back. "That'll be Marjorie, wanting to chat," Jack's mum said. "I'll be back in a moment. Molly, it's your turn for a bath. There should be hot water still in the kettle." She wrapped the tin in the brown paper and put it back in her bag, then pulled on her boots and her coat, and hurried out through the kitchen to the back garden.

Robbie and Jack stared at the bag Mrs. Park had left by the chair in front of the fire.

"Don't," Molly commanded.

"I didn't do anything!" Jack protested.

"Your sister is psychic," Robbie said, laughing. "You should set up a stand at fairs, Molly, and tell people what will happen to them. Make a fortune."

A different girl might have stuck her tongue out at Robbie, but Molly took him seriously. "I would never do that. What if I saw something terrible in their future? What would I tell them?"

"Do you see anything terrible in my future, O wise one?"

Molly regarded Robbie. "You will go to prison, but it will never be for long."

Jack guffawed, as much at the look on Robbie's face as at his sister's words. "She told you, mate," he said, still chuckling, as Molly passed through to the kitchen, where the kettle and tin bath awaited, shutting the door behind her.

Robbie shrugged, though Jack could see he was rattled by her prediction. "She'd make a terrible fortune-teller. Now," he nodded toward the bag, pointedly changing the subject. "Fancy a cigarette?"

"No luck there. Mum doesn't smoke."

"No, you know . . ."

"What, from the tin? We can't do that!"

"Sure we can. Didn't you see? The packet is open at one end—you can see all the cigarettes inside. It'd be easy to pull one out."

"Mum would kill us!"

"Your mum'll never notice. She won't open the tin again. And even if she does, she's not going to count the cigarettes. They're packed in tight—no one will see that one's missing."

"But—" Jack wanted to say that what really bothered him

wasn't his mother's reaction, but the fact that they would be stealing cigarettes from a soldier—from his father, for instance. Even though his father didn't smoke, it wasn't right. Somehow, though, it was hard to say so to Robbie without his friend making fun of him. Besides, they had been talking about trying cigarettes for months. Now they had their chance.

"We'll just take one," Robbie added. "No one will notice. Not even the soldier who gets the tin. They've got bags of cigarettes anyway up at the front."

Jack wasn't sure this was true.

"Come on."

"You do it."

"I couldn't touch your mum's bag!"

When Jack still hesitated, Robbie added, "You get the tin out from the bag, and I'll do the rest."

That seemed easier—at least Jack wouldn't have to touch the soldier's packet of cigarettes. After glancing at the kitchen door that hid his sister from them, he knelt by the chair and pulled open Mrs. Park's bag. The rustling he made as he looked for the tin among his mum's purse and tissues and bits of paper and whatever it was she kept in there was so loud, he was amazed Molly didn't come running in from the kitchen to catch him. Finally his fingers closed around a rectangle. Jack grabbed the tin and handed it to Robbie. Then he closed the bag and went to stand in front of the kitchen door.

"Don't come in!" Molly shouted from behind it, the sound of sloshing water accompanying her.

"I'm not!"

Jack watched as Robbie undid the brown paper, opened the tin, took out the Christmas card, and laid it aside. Then he picked up the yellow packet, pinched the end of a cigarette, and pulled it out. Several came along with it.

"Careful!" Jack hissed.

"What?" Molly called.

"Nothing!"

"Jack, old boy, you worry too much." Robbie pushed back all but two cigarettes.

"I thought you said one," Jack whispered.

"One each."

"No, just one!"

Then he heard his mum call from the kitchen, "See you tomorrow, Marjorie!"

"Quick!" he hissed. "Put it back!"

"All right, all right." Robbie pushed one of the cigarettes back into the packet and slid the other into his pocket. Then he popped the packet back in the tin, shut the lid, wrapped the brown paper around it, and put it in Mrs. Park's bag— all in the ten seconds it took her to shut the back door and come through the kitchen to poke her head into the sitting room.

"Robbie, your mum'll be expecting you back now, won't she?" she said to the two boys warming their hands by the fire.

"I like it better here, Mrs. P."

Jack's mother smiled. "Lovely. Now, get on home with you!"

Only as Robbie was crossing the room did Jack notice Princess Mary's Christmas card lying on the arm of the chair where Robbie had left it. Jack froze and tried to hold himself back. But the strain was too much: after a moment he dived toward the card.

"Jack, what's the matter with you?" his mum cried.

Luckily Robbie was quick to understand, and promptly tripped over his own feet so that he went flying into the umbrella stand by the door, knocking it over and spilling umbrellas everywhere.

"Oh, Robbie, you clumsy boy!" Mrs. Park rushed over to help him up. "Are you all right?"

"Sure, Mrs. P.—Mum always says I'm a bull in a china shop. Sorry about your umbrellas." Robbie set the stand upright and began putting the umbrellas back.

His friend's distraction gave Jack the opportunity to grab the Christmas card. Unfortunately the noise also drew his sister—Molly appeared in the doorway, her hair wrapped in a towel, just as Jack slid the card into his back pocket. Jack stared at her. Molly had taken off her glasses to wash her hair, and though she was looking straight at him, it wasn't clear if she had seen the card or not. He could only hope that her eyesight was as bad as her lenses were thick.

That night Jack lay in bed and fretted. Had Molly seen him? Would his mum discover that the Christmas card was missing from the tin? If so, would she then inspect the contents closely and find out that a cigarette was missing as well? How would she punish him?

And if he and Robbie did get away with it—if his mother didn't notice anything—what about the soldier receiving the tin? Now he wouldn't get a Christmas card. Which in a way was worse than a missing cigarette. He would get no encouraging words from Princess Mary, or her photograph, while others all around him did. Jack recalled the Christmases when he had compared the presents Molly received with his own, and how indignant he had felt if he thought his parents had given her more than him. The soldier might feel the same way.

At last, knowing that he couldn't sleep until he had fixed at least part of the problem, Jack got up as quietly as he could, took the Christmas card from his trouser pocket, and crept downstairs. It was very dark, with the only light coming from the glowing coals in the fireplace, but he didn't dare to light a lamp. Instead he fumbled blindly around in his mother's bag, which was still sitting next to the chair by the fire, and found the tin. It was only when he had it halfway out of its brown wrapping that he heard the sound of a throat being cleared.

Jack looked up and started at the sight of the outline of his sister, sitting very still in the other chair. Now that he could see Molly, he was surprised he hadn't noticed her immediately. She was still wearing a towel around her hair like a turban, and her white nightgown glowed in the dim light. Her spectacles flashed when she moved her head.

Jack did not cry out, or jump up, or begin to make excuses. He sat back on his heels, the tin on the floor in front of him, closed his eyes, and sighed.

Then Molly surprised him. She did not ask what he was doing. Instead she said, "I've been thinking about Dad."

Jack opened his eyes. "What about him?"

"I've been thinking that that tin," she nodded at the tin between them, "will be very handy for storing the letters he gets from us, to keep them from getting wet. I like to think of our letters to him being safe and dry."

Jack nodded. He opened the tin and placed the Christmas card inside. Then he closed it and for the last time wrapped it in the brown paper and put it back in his mother's bag. Instead of going back to bed, however, he sat down in the other chair.

Molly said nothing about the card, and he was grateful. "There's a cigarette missing from the packet in the tin," he said. It was a relief to confess, even if it was just to his sister. "Robbie and I took it."

Molly did not speak, and her expression did not change.

"I—I want to ask Clara something."

"What?"

"What's going to happen to the soldier who receives that tin? Will he be all right?"

Molly looked at him for so long that Jack began to wonder if she was asleep with her eyes open. Then she said, "Clara will tell you." She closed her eyes and began to speak in a small, high voice Jack had never heard before.

"His name was Jimmy, but his nickname in the trenches was Sparky, which was how the other soldiers teased him for not smoking. Sparky had never liked smoking — it hurt his lungs and made him feel dizzy. But he understood the appeal of a little stick of warmth and comfort in the midst of the chaos and carnage of war. He did understand.

Sparky was popular because anytime he was sent cigarettes — people forgot that Sparky didn't smoke; they just assumed all soldiers did — he would give them away.

When Sparky received a Christmas tin from Princess Mary, the thing he liked best wasn't the card from the princess or the photo of her, or the bullet-shaped pencil. Or, of course, the yellow packets of tobacco and cigarettes. It was the tin itself. Every time he held it, he thought of people back home — not just his family and friends and neighbors, but strangers on the street, even the man or woman who had packed the tin for him. It was nice to know that they were all thinking of him and wishing him well. It made Sparky feel he was part of a larger thing — a community that looked out for one another.

At first he didn't do anything with the tin except admire it. Some of the men he was with in the trenches smoked one cigarette from the yellow packet so that they could say they had used the gift, and then sent the tin and all its contents back home as a souvenir. But Sparky kept his, and got out the card and read it and looked at the photo of Princess Mary. He began to use the pencil for writing his letters home. He gave the packet of tobacco to his commanding officer, who liked to smoke a pipe. He kept photos of his wife and children — a boy and a girl — in the tin, where they were safe and dry. He left the cigarettes in there too, saving them for when they were needed most.

That moment came four months later. Sparky was sitting in a trench with the other men in his unit, waiting in the rain for a command. They had waited for hours, getting wetter and muddier and more miserable by the minute. When Sparky looked along the trench at all the unhappy faces, he knew that now was the moment. He took out the tin from a pocket in his uniform, opened it, and removed the yellow packet. Then he started down the trench, offering a cigarette to each soldier. They looked up at him in surprise and gratitude. That little moment of comfort was just what they needed.

The twentieth man — a boy, really, only a few years older than Sparky's son — reached into the packet and frowned. 'None left!'

'Strange — I thought there were twenty in the packet,' Sparky said. 'Sorry, son.'

The boy looked so mournful that Sparky couldn't bear to disappoint him. 'Hang on a minute, I'll get you one.' He started back down the trench, making his way with difficulty through the mud and the crouching men, all the way to where he kept his kit. He thought there might be a spare cigarette in his things.

Sparky was just rummaging through his pack when he heard the explosion — a mortar shell that killed all the men he had just given his cigarettes to, and the boy."

Molly opened her eyes.

Jack shivered, and not just because it was cold without a fire.

A few weeks after Christmas, the Parks received a letter from Jack and Molly's dad:

December 30, 1914
My dear family,

I hope you had a good Christmas, even though I could not be there with you. It was quiet in the trenches for once, and that was a Christmas present in itself.

Thank you for the package, which was much appreciated, especially the Christmas cake, which I shared with the others. They say I am a lucky man to have a wife who bakes so well. I know I am.

Thank you for the socks you knitted, Molly — though the pattern is eccentric, they will certainly keep me warm during winter. And for the knife, Jack — I needed a new one, as the old one was lost in the mud.

I also received a Christmas tin from Princess Mary, as did the other men. They are much admired, and the tin will come in handy. In fact, I am using the pencil from the tin to write to you. Some of the men have sent their tins home, and others have already smoked all their cigarettes. Though there were tins full of chocolate for nonsmokers, those had run out by the time they reached me, so I have cigarettes as well. The others find this funny and have begun calling me "Sparky." I am saving mine for when they are needed most.

Your loving husband and father,
Jim "Sparky" Park

"Lovely letter," Jack's mum said. "Glad he got his package, and his tin." She glanced at her children. Jack was staring at Molly. His sister stared back, her eyes wide as an owl's. "Molly? Jack? Whatever's the matter?"

Jack cleared his throat. "Er, nothing, Mum. Nothing. We're just glad Dad's all right. That Dad's going to be all right."

Previous page: **WOMEN WORKING IN A MUNITIONS FACTORY**
By the end of the war, munitions factories in Britain employed 950,000 women and those in Germany employed 700,000 women. All of these women risked their lives by working with poisonous substances without protective clothing. Two hundred British women died in munitions factories during the war.

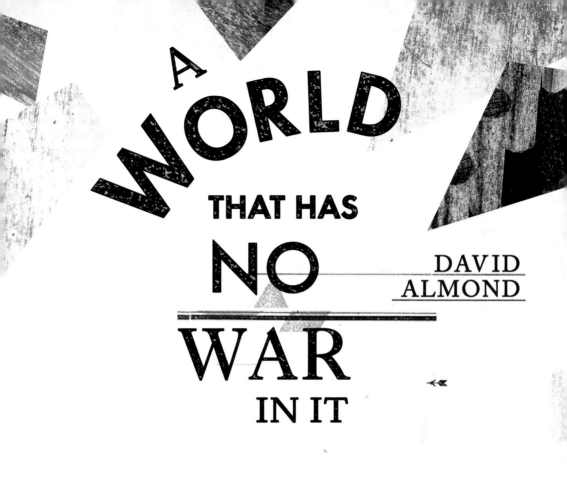

A WORLD THAT HAS NO WAR IN IT

DAVID ALMOND

It had a war in it, the world when I was young. It was the war between the Killens and the Craigs. They lived among us, in the old row houses around the town square, in the streets of 1930s homes, in the new developments growing across the hillside at the eastern edge of town.

The war was normal, just part of growing up round here. Aye, everybody was fed up with it, but hardly anybody dared to say a word.

"It's been going on forever, son," said me dad. "They battled when I was a bairn, and they'll battle till the day of doom. A bunch of nutters. Keep your head down, same as I did when I was a lad."

The kids were the worst. Aye, the blokes had fistfights outside the Wheatsheaf down beyond the railway line. There were brawls on Friday nights at the back of the Black Bull. There was always at least one of them in the Queen Elizabeth Hospital and another one or two in Durham Jail. The women shouted and went at each other on the High Street, too. But the kids! They were the worst. Running through the streets in broad daylight, hoying rocks and half-bricks at each other. Wailing and howling like banshees. Ambushing each other in back lanes, setting traps and trip wires in Holly Hill Park. And the battles! Those great gang fights up on the high fields, bairns from five to fifteen screeching and howling at each other. Bin lids for shields and buckets for helmets and war paint on faces. Aye, it looked daft, but there was nothing daft about the wooden spears they carried, nor the half-bricks and the knuckle-dusters and the blood and the wounds. There was hardly one of them without marks on their face where a rock had hit. And there was little Matt Craig with the limp, Dolly Killen with the twisted arm where a break had badly healed, Russell Craig with three whole fingers missing. What was it? Why did they keep on? What drew them to it and kept on drawing them to it?

Some said it had started way, way back with their ancestors in Ireland. Some said they were all descendants of the ancient Reivers, and all this had been going on since the Border raids. Some said, *What's the point of trying to explain it? They're not like other folk. It's their nature, just the way they are. They're the Killens and the Craigs. They go to war because they love to be at war.*

Sometimes the police made a show, striding through the development with their helmets on and their truncheons in their hands and Alsatians growling at their sides. They knocked on doors, wrote down names, gave out cautions and dire warnings. No use. A Craig wouldn't snitch on a Killen; a Killen wouldn't snitch on a Craig. And who else was going to speak out? There were times when the coppers took a lad or two down a dark back lane and gave them a damn good thumping, but there were no complaints about that. A seeing-to by the law was just part of it all. The warriors bore the scars of that just like they bore their other wounds, with pride.

So war was everywhere, not just in the battles and the scars, but in all that graffiti. Curses painted on garage walls. Six-foot-high obscenities. Dates and names of battles and heroes, some from ages back:

STONEYGATE 1954
THE BATTLE OF HIGH LANES 62

REMEMBER THE HAYNING 1927!
R.I.P. TASH KILLEN
TRUEST OF US ALL
IMLA CRAIG WILL RISE AGAIN.

Weird thing is, some of it was beautiful. There was that strange, ancient-looking lovely lettering they sometimes used. There were those paintings of the Craig girls that appeared on the flagstones of the Sullivan Street pavements that time. Aye, they were brutal, but everybody could see how lovely the shapes were, how *artistic* it was. Like cave paintings or something, somebody said, or like those paintings of Saint Catherine and Saint Lucy in Saint Patrick's church. And there was that famous mural on the walls of the old railway tunnel underneath the bypass, the one that showed all the Craigs dangling from ropes, their necks snapped. Must have taken days to make. It was in many colors. It was accompanied by poems and prayers for the fallen and hymns in praise for the victors. And above it all was a painted banner:

WE WILL PRAY FOR OUR
ENEMIES WHEN THEY ARE GONE.

It stayed there for months. There was always talk of scraping it off, painting over it, but nobody did. Loads of folk came to try to take photographs of it. And the Craigs themselves were seen there, with torches, picking out their own faces and those of their fathers, and smiling, and snarling, and clenching their fists, and laughing as they promised bloody retribution.

It added to the weirdness of it all. Some said the Craigs and the Killens must be stupid, going on the way they did, but it was clear that they weren't. They just loved their war, and who knows where it would have ended if it hadn't been for two kids falling in love, for the visit of Agnes Bourne, and for the death of poor little May McShane?

The lad I knew best was Danny Craig. I'd been at school with him since Mrs. Fagan's class, when we were five years old. He was a little wiry kid who already had a sickle-shaped scar on his left cheek. We did our first palm prints and scatter paintings together. One time we turned the surface of our desk into a planet and made Plasticine aliens and spacemen and spaceships. We told a story about the spacemen being lost in space and asking the aliens the way home. The aliens wanted to be very helpful, but they knew nothing about Earth or how to get there. We laughed as we raised the aliens up and held them beside our faces and made them speak in weird voices.

"Stay here with us, earthlings," said Danny's alien. "We'll

look after you. It's lovely and peaceful, much nicer than your world. You do not have to struggle or fight. Have some ice cream and cake."

Danny was so clever; he learned so fast. It was like he could do anything. As we moved up the infant and junior school, I saw how he could run streams of words together into sentences, pages, stories, poems. He raced through sums and problems. He could paint and draw, and he kept on making amazing things with Plasticine. At Christmas and on our visits to church, he sang like an angel. He ran like a deer, played football like a star. I never sat at his side again after Mrs. Fagan's, but I could see he wanted to stay close. A few times he asked me if I wanted to go swimming or something with him. One day he even asked if I wanted to come to his place for tea. But I always found a reason why it wasn't possible. Not a good idea, to become a friend of a Craig. I admired him from a distance, and I kept the distance. Aye, he could be all sweetness and light in school, but I'd seen the wild boy in him in the streets and parks and fields outside. And I'd never forget that day when we were nine, in Mrs. Henry's class.

I watched him sharpen his pencil under his desk with a penknife. He kept glancing at me, like he wanted me to see. He looked back at me as he took it out into the yard at playtime, like he wanted me to follow. I did, and I was the only one who saw him move smoothly to the back of ten-year-old Wilfred

Killen. I saw his arm suddenly jerk forward, heard Wilfred's cry, saw the pencil sticking out of Wilfred's leg as Danny spun away.

He calmly met my eye as he came back into the room after the useless inquisition by the headmaster, after Wilfred had been driven to the hospital by Mr. Mulvaney. He sat down and picked up his books. He knew I was still watching, and he calmly turned to me, like he'd done something to me and not just to Wilfred.

"It's them and us," he murmured, "and war."

And he shrugged and got on with his work.

At the time I'm writing of, we were twelve, just turning thirteen. We were in grammar school, and it was 1964. His dad was in the hospital; not one of the wounded, but some lung infection, we had heard. Danny'd been top of the class the year before. He had a painting of a sailing ship in the school entrance hall and another of a kestrel in the headmaster's office.

We were doing lots of stuff about the fiftieth anniversary of the First World War, and one day Danny got up in assembly and recited "Anthem for Doomed Youth" in front of the whole school.

> "Not in the hands of boys, but in their eyes
> Shall shine the holy glimmers of good-byes.
> The pallor of girls' brows shall be their pall."

He spoke it like a song, and it was so lovely, and so weird, coming from a lad with H ATE and LOVE tattooed into his knuckles and a brand-new jagged scar on his bright young face. The teachers sighed at how beautiful it was. The Killen kids twisted their faces and muttered in disgust. Alice Killen was close behind me. I turned around. Her eyes were on Danny Craig, her enemy, and they burned with love.

Some of us had known for months. We knew the way they looked at each other. There were whispers, rumors.

"They were walkin' together on that paddock down by the Tyne. . . ."

"I seen them at the far end of the beach at Shields. . . ."

"It was them, in the dark part of the field at Swards Road. . . ."

"They were kissin'. . . ."

"No!"

"Aye, they were!"

We would have teased and mocked anyone else. But not these two.

"Hush. . . ."

"Keep it quiet. . . ."

"Keep a distance. . . ."

We kept on watching, waiting. Could it have been love, at such an age? Who knows? We'd all found ourselves looking at lads and lasses in a different way. Claudia Wilson had once or twice caused my own heart to skip a beat. But my true love was still for my football boots, for running round with the lads on the fields yelling, "On me heed! On me heed!" But Danny was more mature than me, and probably Alice was as well, and mebbe their love was intensified by the fact that the only thing they were supposed to feel for each other was hate.

It all blew up, of course. None of us snitched. Didn't need to. All the whispers, all the rumors, all the glances. No way to keep it hidden in our little world. The Killens and the Craigs found out.

The story was that Danny's brothers and cousins tied him up one night. They took him down to the quiet patch at the far end of Heworth Graveyard. They knocked him about and threatened him with rocks and razors. They tied a rope around his neck and yelled, "Is this what you want? We're warnin' ye, it's what'll happen." A couple of the blokes were there but just as observers. It's said they only backed off because of Danny's dad being in hospital.

And Alice? It seems the Killens took her to an aunt who lived over the water in Wallsend. She was a witch or a medium or something. She cast spells on the lass, stuck weird needles into her, gave her some potion or other, told her to cast out the evil from herself. They threatened to send her away to some far-flung part of the family in County Cork.

Danny and Alice were two determined kids. The trouble just drew them closer. They got more open. They walked hand in hand through the sunshine together. They hung about with each other in the school yard. We heard of the thumpings Danny got at home, of the intensifying threats that were made to Alice.

One day I was walking behind Danny after school along Stanhope Street when a whole bunch of Killens appeared. They caught him, kicked him to the ground, and kept on kicking him. I heard the thud of their boots on his body.

One of them caught me staring.

"What you looking at?"

I could hardly speak.

"You'll kill him," I squawked.

"Stop it!" I stammered.

They laughed.

"Keep your eyes off her!" they yelled at him. "Keep your hands off her."

They kicked again. Then Thompson the butcher ran out of his shop, and they all scattered. The butcher helped Danny to his feet as I moved away.

A couple of days later, Danny came to me in the school yard. He was limping. There were bruises on his face, a gash in his cheek. He grinned.

"Thanks," he said.

"For what?" I muttered.

I saw the Killens watching. I was already backing away.

"Do you want to . . . ?" he started. "What's wrong?"

"Nowt," I said.

I kept my head down.

"I don't want to get involved," I whispered.

"What?"

"Nowt."

The Killens laughed as I passed close by.

"Coward," I whispered to myself.

Later that day, we were talking in class about First World War poets.

"So many of them died so young," said the teacher we called the Mop. "So many futures stifled. So many stars put out." He leaned toward us. "You are such fortunates," he said. "What will you do with your good fortune? What will you do with your lives?"

Danny raised his hand.

"Make a new world, sir," he answered.

"It looks like you need to," said the Mop. "What kind of world?"

"A world where things like that can't happen again, sir. A world where people don't *let* things like that happen."

And he looked at me, and I looked away.

It was the love and bravery of those two kids that led to the last great and tragic battle. It took place on Leam Lane Estate, that great growth of houses, gardens, and parks spread out across the hill to the east of town. An early summer Saturday. A sunny afternoon. Lots of folk out in the streets and gardens. Kids picnicking on the grass. Sun beating down on the pale pavements. I walked through the heat to the great triangular green below Fossfeld. I had a new Newcastle United football top on. A bunch of the lads were already there. They had jumpers down for goalposts and a match was already under way. I saw Danny and Alice sitting together on a garden wall nearby. I ran onto the turf and raced toward the ball. The teams surged back and forth across the pitch.

There was the sound of a drum being beaten. Chanting echoed across the roofs. Then they came, the Killen kids from the streets at the bottom edge of the green, the Craigs from the streets at the top. They had the rocks and sticks and the stupid helmets and armor and shields. They were even carrying tattered flags, like this was some great battle from King Arthur's day. The Killens had a banner: **NO RETREAT.** The Craigs' said: **NO FORGIVENESS.** A couple of blokes went toward them. "Not here! Not today! Do your stupid fighting somewhere else."

Made no difference. Straightaway the two armies were running across the green, screaming and yelling. It looked so damn ridiculous—little bairns hardly out of nappies, skinny kids in shorts, twelve-year-olds in winklepickers and jeans, fifteen-year-olds with their first fuzz of beards, feathers in their hair and war paint on their faces. It was like they were trying to be an army of ancient warriors, in this new estate in a little insignificant town. It was like some mad cartoon. Folk rushed inside, slammed their doors. Footballers and picnickers scattered.

Danny and Alice didn't budge. They sat on the wall and watched. Mebbe they were the ones that found it stupidest of all. They watched the thumping and the brawling and waited for it to be over.

Then it happened. There was a scream right from the middle of it, higher and more terrifying than any other scream. A scream that pierced right through it all, a scream that didn't stop. And the message got through to all the fighting fools, and they started backing off, leaving a space in the center where there was just Dorothy McShane kneeling where her little sister May lay, already dead.

A half-brick. A stupid half-brick. It missed what it was supposed to hit. It hit a lovely young bairn on a bright summer morning on Fossfeld Green. And we all gathered in a wide circle around her, and there among us were Alice Killen and Danny Craig, hand in hand, and both in tears.

And then the ambulance, and then the police, and then the silence. And the shock of it all, but no real damn surprise.

Nobody knew who had chucked it. Even the one who threw it probably didn't know. Aye, there was a fuss. The police came banging on doors and making their threats. They brought their snarling dogs. They came in to school a week after May's death. Three of them. They stood on the stage beside the headmaster, and they were massive in their dark uniforms and their high helmets and their big black boots. A statue of the Virgin Mary looked down on them from a niche in the wall. They showed their truncheons. They dangled handcuffs. They jangled a big set of keys they said came straight from Durham Jail. They even held up a hangman's noose, and all of us shuddered at that.

"This is what lies in wait for them that break the law. This is what violence will bring you to. We will impose the law in the streets of this town. We will make you suffer. We will come down *hard*."

They glared. They left the stage. They muscled their way through us toward the door. They looked with contempt at the Killens and the Craigs. I saw Danny gazing back at them, his own eyes all defiance, and farther back was Alice, her mouth twisted in scorn.

"Attention!" came the command from the stage. "Eyes this way!"

Hitler, a little dark-haired Latin teacher, stood there holding his black strap.

"We will stand with the guardians of the law," he snarled. "The time of misrule is over. Do you hear? *Over*."

He brought the strap down hard upon an imaginary hand.

"This will be a place of *peace*!" He glared into the silence. "Do you *understand*? You had better, or you will be *sorry*. Now listen to the words of your headmaster."

He stepped aside. The headmaster came to the front.

"Thank you, Mr. Butcher," he said.

And he told us that we'd be visited next week by Agnes Bourne.

She was coming with yet more stuff about the First World War. We were fed up with it: all those poems; Wilfred Owen, Rupert Brooke; all the faded pictures of the trenches and the troops; Kitchener pointing out from the posters; the lists of the battles; the Western Front; the dreadful Somme; the whizzbangs and the rats; "Pack Up Your Troubles in Your Old Kit Bag"; and wouldn't it be great to be in Tipperary. Aye, we knew all that, and we knew it had been dreadful and we knew how lucky we were to live in a different age. But it *was* a different age. We lived in modern times. Time to do something more relevant.

A few classes were put together in the hall. Hitler and the Mop were there. *Be gentle when she arrives,* they said. She'd been born in 1893. 1893! Hell's teeth! She'd be withered and stooped, she'd stink of pee and have drool at the corners of her mouth. But no. Here came a quick little woman with dark-red hair and bright-green eyes and a silver bangle on each wrist. She laughed quick and easy, and her voice was light and fresh. You could see that, aye, she might be old, but a child lived on in her.

"Were you *really* born in 1893?" said Tex Blake.

"Was that in Tudor times?" called somebody else.

Hitler scowled, but Agnes laughed.

"Much further back than *that*!" she said.

She had a big red handbag with her. She clicked it open and took out an envelope and a little battered box.

"I told your headmaster I'd show you this," she said, "and that I'd tell you about John."

She took a little photograph out of the envelope. "Come in close to see him right," she said.

We gathered round. She held it up and moved it around so all of us could see. The picture was faded and cracked. But we saw the bright eyes of the young man gazing calmly out at us.

"He's *bonny*, miss," said Carrie King.

Agnes looked straight at Danny Craig.

"A bonny lad like this one, eh?"

"Did he die, miss?" someone asked.

The obvious question. Why else would she be showing him to us?

"Oh, yes," said Agnes. "It's what happens in a war."

"Did you love him, miss?"

This time it was the eyes of Alice that she caught.

"Wouldn't *you*?" she said.

"Oh, yes, miss!' said Alice softly back.

"Yes, indeed," said Agnes. "I loved him with all my heart."

"Was he a hero, miss?" asked one of the boys.

"Oh, *all* the boys and young men were heroes."

"*Was* he, miss?"

She put the photograph on the desk before her.

"He was an ordinary lad like you are," she said. "He became an ordinary young man as you will. And like too many ordinary folk, he believed too many lies."

She pointed to the poster on the wall: Kitchener's face, his pointing finger:

YOUR COUNTRY NEEDS YOU

"He believed the *king* needed him and that God himself needed him to go."

"Did *you* believe that, miss?"

She sipped her tea.

"We all did. They told us what to believe. They told us we were good and the enemy was bad and God was on our side."

"Do you *believe* in God, miss?" I asked.

Hitler frowned and glared at me. A crucifix hung from the wall above his head.

"I believe that we are daft," said Agnes. "I believe that we can be made to believe the most infernal claptrap. Now, look."

She took out a sheet of paper wrapped in cellophane. It was a letter, written on the finest, frailest, almost translucent paper. The writing on it was faded, almost gone, but we could see the shapes of letters and words and paragraphs.

"The officers often wrote in pen, and their words have lasted better," she said. "But do you see the words? *Agnes. Cold.* That says *Memory.* And look there. You see? That says *Love.* And there is *John.*"

"That's lovely, miss," said Doreen Cairns.

"It is. He'd tried poetry, but he said he couldn't find a rhyme for Agnes. And there's this — look."

Another sheet of paper, this time with drawings on it. They were faded like the writing, but Agnes guided us to see the shapes of a trench, the shape of a soldier bearing a rifle, the shape of another lying dead on barbed wire.

"Aren't they lovely?" she said. She peered at us. "But how can it be that something so awful can be lovely as well? Answer me that."

Nobody did. She showed us another drawing, of a lovely young woman with dark eyes.

"You?" asked someone.

"Yes. Me."

"That *is* lovely, miss."

"Were you going to marry him, miss?"

"Yes. And we were going to have two boys and two girls and a Jack Russell and a cocker spaniel."

She refolded the papers.

"He wrote this and drew those on a bitter winter morning in a trench in France. He put them into an envelope. And that very same day, he died."

"That's awful, miss."

"Yes. It is."

She sighed and lifted the little box she'd brought.

"This," she said, "was his writing case. This is where he kept his pencils and his paper. It found its way back to me, months after he was gone."

She opened it carefully. It was a simple thing. There was an ancient eraser, hard as stone, a rolled-up sheet of blue paper. And five pencils, resting in slots. They were a few inches long, cracked; the paint on them had flaked away; each of them was almost blunt.

"One of these must be the actual pencil with which he drew me and expressed his love for me. This one, perhaps. Or this. Sometimes I write with them and try to feel his spirit in them. Sometimes I think that I really do. Do you think that's possible?"

"Yes," some murmured.

"Yes, and maybe you'll feel his spirit, if you choose to write with them."

"Us, miss?"

"Yes, you. You could write with them, just like he did in the trenches on the day he died."

Some shuddered at the idea.

"If you choose to, of course," she said.

"I will, miss," said Alice Killen.

"And me," said Danny Craig.

Two more volunteered.

"And me," I said.

She took out a penknife.

"I sharpen them rarely or they will just pass away." She smiled. "As I will, soon enough."

She asked Danny his name. She passed him the pencils and the knife.

"Sharpen them gently, Danny. The wood is distressed. The graphite is frail. Cut very little away from them."

I watched him sharpen these ancient things, so gently, one by one. He looked into my eyes as he passed me mine. He still had yellow bruises on his face. The gash was turning to a scar. I held the pencil between my fingers while Agnes gave out sheets of thin blue paper and asked the others to write with their own pens. I closed my eyes and tried to imagine that this was fifty years ago, that I was the soldier holding the pencil.

"What should we write, miss?" said Alice.

Her voice was soft. She sat very close to Danny. Their shoulders touched.

"John wanted to be a poet," said Agnes. "So maybe you could write a poem. He wrote about love, so maybe you could write about love. He wrote about war, as he was bound to, and maybe you will find that you must also write about war."

She laughed bitterly.

"That won't be hard," she said. "He died in the war that was supposed to end all wars. Ha! And ever since, there's been war after war and death after death and the same old stupid lies! It's 1964, a time of peace, and war is all around us. They are evil and we are good! God is on our side. There are bombs enough to kill us all. We are idiots. The armies grow, the bombs are built, young men are trained to kill and die."

She shook her head, composed herself.

"My John," she said softly, "said that he wanted to write stories that had no war in them, poems that had no war in them, to draw pictures that had no war in them. He wanted to come back home and to make a world that had no war in it."

Hitler brought her a cup of tea, and her hand trembled slightly as she raised it to her lips.

"Do that, children. Use John's pencils. Use your pens. Write a world that has no war in it. You're young. Be brave. Be proper heroes. Write a world that's better than the world before."

We wrote. The silence and concentration in the room seemed to flow from Agnes herself. There was the scraping of pencils, of ballpoints, of pens. We sighed as we worked. Sometimes we gazed into empty space. Agnes would meet our eyes, nod, smile gently. Hitler and the Mop seemed removed from it all.

Did I feel the spirit of the soldier in me? Not at first. I tried to write of a world without war, but my words kept turning to little May McShane, to the pencil in Wilfred Killen's leg, to war paint and half-bricks, to the strangely beautiful mural under the bypass. I found myself writing about Russia and the USA and about atomic bombs. Then I turned back to our little world and wrote about the noise and the excitement of the battles on the high fields, the chanting and the screams and the banging of drums, about war paint and brawls and wounds and scars. It was all so bright, so vivid, and so exciting to find the words to fit the battles. The pencil raced across the page. Then I stopped myself. *Hell's teeth,* I wrote. *Maybe it's not just the Killens and the Craigs that love their war. Maybe I love it, too.* And I let the pencil fall, and then something did rush into me. Not words, but feelings, sensations, excitement, dread. There was icy air on my face and the stench of filth and acrid smoke in my nostrils. The room rocked with the thud of explosions. I heard deep groans of pain, high yells of terror. I opened my mouth to scream myself, but it was just a moment; then it was gone.

When I looked up, Agnes was drinking with a wobbly hand.

"You all right, dear?" she whispered.

I nodded.

"You sure?"

I nodded.

Others looked up now, as if surprised to find themselves there.

"That was amazing, miss," said little Susan Muldoon.

Agnes smiled.

"It's never been like that," said Malcolm Ross.

He looked at what he'd written as if he was astonished by it.

"I was *there,*" whispered Thomas Bell.

"Would you like to tell us what you wrote about?" said Agnes. "You don't have to if you don't want to."

"I wrote about war," I said. "I'm sorry."

"That's all right. I said you might have to. Someone else?"

"I wrote a letter to the prime minister, telling him to keep us out of any wars."

"I wrote about how sad God is when he looks at the awful things that happen on his Earth."

"I wrote a love letter, miss," said Alice Killen.

I looked across, saw the neat writing, the beautifully shaped paragraphs. I saw Alice's eyes shining. Agnes winked.

"I won't ask who the lucky boy is," she said.

"I wrote about another world," Danny quickly said. "The

aliens who live there have no wars. They don't understand us. *Why can't you just get along with each other?* they say. And I drew a picture."

He held it up. It was of Alice, of course.

Agnes sighed.

"Pastoral poetry, political statements, theology, love letters, science fiction! And war, of course. See how abundant our imaginations are!"

She sipped her tea.

We could see that she was tiring, brightness fading in her eyes, her voice now turning frail.

She said she'd gather up the pencils now. I scribbled one last sentence.

Before she left, she told us, "Be proper heroes, children. Tell your children to be proper heroes, too. Be brave, and change the world."

And she was gone.

I took a breath. I composed myself. I dared myself.

I pushed the piece of paper into Danny's hand. He showed it to Alice. They looked at me together.

"I'm sorry," I said.

"OK," he said. "I'll be your friend."

Danny went on writing in the days that followed. He wrote with Alice in the library at lunchtimes. Our friendship was a precarious thing, and I knew that he didn't truly trust me. But he asked me to look at their work.

"I felt him in me," he said.

"John?"

"Yes, the soldier. I felt that I was writing for him."

I could see that he didn't think that I'd believe him.

"That's great," I said.

"And I felt Dorothy McShane," said Alice, "as she knelt at her sister's side."

It was a letter to all the Killens and the Craigs.

The time of war is over, I read. *It is time for peace.*

I said they were doing a bold and brilliant thing.

"Will you come with us?" asked Alice.

"Come where?"

"Will you help us to deliver the letter to them all?"

I caught my breath at the thought of going to such places with these two people.

We have to be brave, I read. *We have to be proper heroes.*

"It will make a difference," she said. "They'll see that everyone can work together."

This can't go on. All of us are damaged by it.

I dared myself. I shivered.

"OK," I said. "I'll come."

And I did. And we spent a whole weekend walking together through the new developments, the streets of 1930s homes, the row houses close to the town square. We carried the words and dreams of two kids who wanted to change the world.

Things did begin to change. They were bound to, of course. The world's forever changing. And we were young, and growing fast.

Time hurried forward as it must, and it's kept on hurrying forward. And fifty years have passed. Fifty years! The First World War's a hundred years ago. The war between the Killens and the Craigs faltered and diminished. Aye, even now there'll be outbursts of contempt on the High Street, a brawl on Friday night behind the Eagle. But they're nothing compared with what took place so long ago. There are hardly any injuries, few scars, no trips to Durham Jail. The graffiti has crumbled, faded, or been scraped entirely away.

Danny and Alice rejected the old lies, and they showed all of us a new kind of truth. They've stayed together ever since, so it must have been true love. They had four kids, two boys and two girls, and they named them the Killen-Craigs. And the kids have gone on to have kids of their own, so peace is spreading on through time.

Danny's stayed my friend as well. He became an artist and an art teacher. He paints and draws and makes amazing murals with troubled kids. He runs a theater group with Alice, and they put on crazy shows in tents all across the North. This year they're doing *Oh, What a Lovely War!* It's about the First World War, of course, but anybody who knows them knows it's about the war between the Killens and the Craigs as well.

I still have the sheet of paper I wrote the day that Agnes Bourne arrived. It's the chronicle of a different age. It's a legend, filled with the thrill and the drama, the sights and the sounds of ancient battle. I once told Danny that. I told him about how exciting it sometimes seemed to kids who weren't involved.

"Aye," he said. "But that's because you weren't involved. It's because you didn't know how bliddy awful it was for us who were."

Agnes Bourne died just a few months after her visit. We hadn't known it, but she was already very ill when she was with us that day. I failed in the task that she set us. We all did. Look around, read the papers, search the Net, watch the news. War in so many places. Bullets flying, shells exploding, armies slaughtering, people dying. Millions and millions of refugees, thousands and thousands of child soldiers. Are we daft? Are we evil? Is it just the way we are? Are we acting out something that started with our ancestors? Is it in our bones and blood? Do we go to war because we're in love with war? Will we be asking those damn questions till the very end of time?

In her will, Agnes left the pencils from John's writing case to the children who had used them that day. So a pencil came to me. I have it still. I use it rarely and sharpen it hardly ever at all. It's a hundred years old now, and it's cracked and blunt and very frail. Sometimes I just hold it and close my eyes and try to feel the spirit of the long-dead soldier. Sometimes I dare to write with it. Very carefully, I wrote parts of this story with it, the very few parts that have no war in them.

Sometimes I take it with me in to schools and tell its story. I ask children to hold it carefully and to allow it to carry them back to a trench in France a hundred years ago. *Make a mark with it*, I say: *a single letter, a single word. Now take your own pen and retain that feeling. Write a poem, a story, a letter, a song. Now try the hardest task of all. Feel the spirit of the long-dead soldier named John in you. Feel Agnes Bourne and Dorothy McShane, and Alice Killen and Danny Craig. Let them speak through you. Go on. Create a better world. Write a world that has no war in it.*

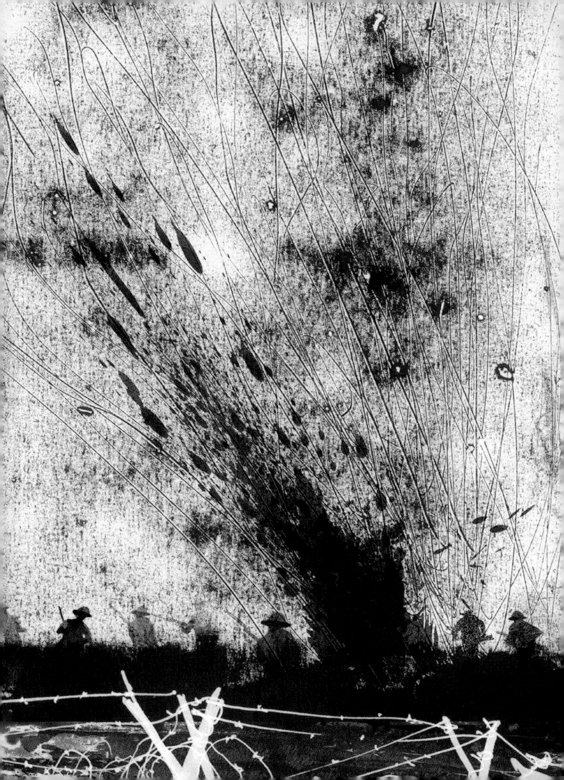

Previous page: **SOLDIERS GOING OVER THE TOP**
Soldiers tried to advance into enemy territory by going "over the top" (out of the trenches into no-man's-land). When they left the trenches, they were completely unprotected from enemy fire. During the four months of the Battle of the Somme in 1916, Germany suffered 465,000 casualties and Allied forces 623,907.

TANYA
LEE STONE

A HARLEM
HELLFIGHTER
AND
HIS
HORN

Let me tell you something.
Music has taken me out of harm's way
more than once—
put me smack in it, too.

Oh yeah,
starting long before I
was making
my own decisions,
my mama stuck a fiddle in my hand,
scraping together the pennies it took
to pay the Music Man
so I could learn something of "value," as she liked to put it,
instead of drumming up trouble with the other boys,
running the streets.
I grumbled, sure, but when I got to be fifteen,
truth be told I was grateful for the excuse on several occasions—
you know nothing trumps the threat of an ass-whooping on the block
more than your mama setting you straight
for an hour or two.

Then there I was, quick as a blink,
nineteen years old,
out from under Mama and doing my best to make something
of myself.

Work was hard to come by in Harlem in 1910.
I had a decent enough gig
at the drugstore, stocking shelves, taking inventory,
sweeping up.

But for music, I might have just stayed there,
keeping time with the
swoosh, swoosh, swoosh
of my push broom
for always.

Maybe making something of yourself is about
not
just keeping time
but *doing* something of substance,
something risky,
something you couldn't fathom having the
skill
guts
nuts
to do until
you
do it.
Not just one thing
or one time
but a steady succession of proving you're more
than you thought
until you actually begin to believe
that you can do
anything.

And maybe sometimes
you need someone
to ask you the right
question.

That's where
James Reese Europe comes in.
Big Jim, to some.
Not to me.
Not ever.
Mr. Europe, James, sir,
Maestro, maybe even,
but Big Jim?
I had too much respect for the man to ever get that
familiar.
Even though I knew something about him
at the time,
I didn't know
little George Gershwin sat outside on a stoop
listening to him play piano,
I didn't know
Vernon and Irene Castle, darlings of dance, invented the
fox-trot craze with him,
and I sure didn't know
how he would set the metronome a-ticking for
the tempo my life would take.

He plucked me off a corner near Morningside Park.
I was on a break,
trying to get some green in my eyes
amid the gray noise of 123rd Street.
I was just standing up against warm bricks,
sassing passersby and whistling some riffs of
"Swing Low, Sweet Chariot."
He walked on by me,
then doubled back,
looked on me square before cocking his right ear:
"Son, can you feel the
boom-da-boom chick-a-chick
rhythm
of this world
you're leaning on so hard?"

The question was not your average
question, oh no.
That's a sit-up-and-take-notice
question.
I give myself some credit. Another boy might have
laughed,
told the old bug-eyed bastard he was crazy,
waved him by.

Another day
I might have too, so, maybe not too much
credit.
But that moment when someone says something to
just the right person at
just the right moment—
that feeling?
That question shot me to the quick,
took the crinkle out of my knees,
stood me up straight,
cocky grin gone,
sass blown right out of me.

I said, simply,
"Yes, sir."

That seemed to amuse him.
He smiled. Slow,
then it crept across his face
like a cat confident he'd caught another tasty critter.

He went in for the kill.
"Got any musical talent?"
Like he could smell it on me. You see what I'm saying here?
Just the right question.
"Matter of fact, I do."

He squinted at me, sunlight bouncing off his spectacles.
"Is that right?"
"Yes, sir, that's right." And I told him about
Mama and the fiddle and the
notes on a clef
just looking right to me somehow.
James Reese Europe laughed out loud at that.

Said I'd fit right in down at the
Clef Club.
That he was looking for professional musicians—that is to say, for pay.
Didn't matter if I'd never played a horn,
I'd pick it up right quick with a proper skill like that, he said.
Put you smack in the middle of one of the groups
like you're the smartest kid in the class,
folks sneaking peeks
at your paper.
Came to find out later there were boys holding instruments
who couldn't read a note,
but they riffed off of me,
and others better trained, smack in the middle of their own small clusters
that all together made up our ranks,
and within weeks—*weeks* I tell you—
the Clef Club orchestra was all kinds of hot.

Headquarters were down on West 53rd
right across from Marshall's Hotel,
a part of Harlem I hadn't met yet,
where New York's "Black Bohemia" and their white friends
gathered for cold drinks and hot jazz,
where Dunbar and Du Bois made noise,
where Bert Williams and George Walker did the cakewalk,
where Ziegfeld found his *Follies* star.

James Reese Europe put our
muster of musicians together,
and oh did we grow
and blow
straight onto the stage of one
Carnegie Hall.
No lie.
The Carnegie Hall.
If that wasn't a million miles from 123rd Street.

And we belonged there,
yes, we did.
You could see it on the faces of the folks — black and white
in the audience, side by side.
First time *that* happened, I tell you that. And oh,
were their eyes open,

wide open,
and their ears were, too.
Oh, they were smiling.
They were smiling big,
So big looked like their teeth were going to burst loose from their
mouths—
we were that
good.

The Clef Club,
That's who we were.
That group meant the world to James Reese Europe.
Why, you should have heard him,
letting any establishment we were about to play
know what was
and what wasn't
going to happen there:
No Clef Club players were going to get
stuck
washing dishes or sweeping up
after we played for the people.

That horn I hadn't known grew part of me,
fused near right to me,
left hand curved around the slide,

right fingers ready on the valves,
the tang of that salty metal mouthpiece on my lips a daily craving,
and all that brass
curling around, cradling my heart.

Mr. Europe, well,
that man knew his music inside and
out,
never looking down,
no, no,
not once.
Sheet music was pretty but
his eyes saw only us,
us, in our finery,
our night-black tuxedos and crisp white shirts,
lifting those notes off the page,
making them
fly.

So when President Wilson put out the call to
"make the world safe for democracy" and join the fight
against Germany,
our leader enlisted,
assembling a regiment band to accompany the 369th —
the Harlem Hellfighters, as we came to be called —

there was no question about it for me.
I followed Europe to
Europe
without taking a beat.
It was like Du Bois said, "If this is our country,
then this is our war."
Never mind there were times that
"If"
hung out there on its own like a lone man
waiting to catch the last train home past midnight.

We were among the first regiments in France.
These soldiers had no beef
standing side by side with us
in the field.
No beef at all.
At first, war seemed glory,
stupidity of youth my only excuse.
Would have joined band or no band,
truth be told.
Would have slung a rifle across my chest instead of a horn,
if I had to.
And sometimes
I had to.
There is accompanying the regiment,

and there is *accompanying* the regiment.
It was war, after all. I have
tripped over men past saving,
fallen to the ground,
scrambled on sharp
elbows and knees to safety,
swapped a horn valve for a trigger in my fingers,
heard gunshots blasting near my ear
like the sharp staccato of a marching drum.

We fought in places with lyrical names like
Château-Thierry and Belleau Wood,
places I couldn't pronounce but could
defend,
pushing those Germans back
five miles through the cold, wet woods.
We did not retreat.
"Go forward or die" was our
command.

Maybe making something of yourself is as
simple
as having the gumption to do something
bigger
than you could have ever

imagined,
of walking, no,
marching
straight into the center of
fear
all while playing a horn,
blowing
your worries
into sweet, bold, triumphant
Music.
Music.
The unrelenting notes drifting out and
up
into the fiery air,
a cacophony of sound,
of jazz that
in any other place would be
raucous joy,
dancing feet,
wild abandon,
mouths wide from not being able to
contain
that sheer merriment of sound,
but here,
here,

in this fearsome, awful place in time,
this war,
this wall of sound
strong as concrete
smacks against
the tat-tat-a-tat, tat-tat-a-tat
of guns popping,
yelps flying,
bullets whizzing,
striking flesh,
here
that raucous sound slams against the wail of a
man down,
horn blares,
brightening the moans
of the dying,
marching band morphing into funeral march.

Maybe making something out of yourself is what you do
in one moment out of millions —
one moment that, if you're not paying attention,
vanishes,
and maybe if you're not paying attention,
you vanish, too.

Because if James Reese Europe
hadn't interrupted my useless afternoon near
Morningside Park,
hadn't dragged me all the way down to West 53rd,
hadn't stuck a horn in my hand,
shown me how to make something
out of not much,
cracked his baton on the metal edge of his stand
and woken me up;
If I
hadn't been marching through fear,
brass against my breast,
that bullet sent to cut me down
would have.
I wouldn't have been able to get back up
far, far from Harlem,
still so part of the rhythm I feel in this earth
I'm leaning on.
A single bullet caught in the heart of my horn,
a hair from my own beating drum,
brass capturing lead,
stopping its blasted path,
letting me
live
another day
to tell you something.

So I won't waste it:
War can break a man.
Slam him down on his back in the
dark.

But music,
Music
can lift him right up off that hard, frigid ground
and carry him somewhere
good.

Previous page: TANK IN A SHELL HOLE

Ten million tons of shells were fired during World War I. Shells were explosive-filled missiles that killed millions of men and left huge gashes in the landscape. Soldiers who were exposed to shellfire were at risk of psychological breakdown known as shell shock.

MAUD'S STORY

ADÈLE GERAS

My name is Maud Evans. Once, a long
time ago, I did something that I want to
write down because I'm proud of what I
did, even though at the time I was terrified
and if I'd been found out, I don't know
what would have happened—not only to
me but to my sister, Ada.

How do you begin to tell a story? Well,
the people in the story come first, don't
they? I think they do. Or maybe the date.
At my school, our teacher, Miss Portham,
always used to write the date on the blackboard. The date today is November 18,
1929, but the story—well, that happened
in 1917.

I was twelve years old then and still at school, though not for very much longer. Soon I'd be going to work, though I tried not to think about that too much because I loved learning and enjoyed reading and writing, and I worried that I wouldn't have the time for such things once I had to earn a wage. I lived in Stoke-on-Trent with my family: my mother, Joan, who worked as a charwoman; my sister, Ada, who was eighteen; and our two brothers, Percy and Alfie. Percy was seven and Alfie was five, and we called them the Little Ones. Our father had died just after Alfie was born, from pneumonia. I can remember how horrible his breath sounded at the end: bubbling and gurgling in his chest. Ada and I used to lie there at night with our pillows over our ears to stop ourselves from hearing that noise.

Ada and I couldn't have been more different. She was short for her age, and not exactly slim, but she had a pretty, merry face, and when our dad was alive, he used to say lamplighters could use Ada's smile to spark up the streetlights. No one said a word about my smile. I was big for my age, and when people spoke about me, it was always, "Watch where you're putting your big feet, Maudie!" or "Am I going to have to turn down that skirt again? When'll you be done growing?" You get used to that sort of thing in the end, and by the time I was twelve, I never even heard the remarks, not properly.

Ada had been stepping out with Stan Althrop since July

1915, almost a year after the beginning of the Great War, when she was sixteen and he was eighteen. Stan was tall and skinny, with a comical sort of face, and they'd met at a fair that Ada had gone to with her friend Sally. They'd been standing in front of the coconut shy, looking in their purses to see if they had any pennies left to spend, when Stan and his chum approached them. As Ada told it to me, he'd offered to pay for her to have a go at hitting a coconut by herself. When she knocked the hairy article for a loop, everyone clapped, and they decided to celebrate with lemonade all around. That was July. By August, the two of them were always together. If you saw Ada, you'd look around to see where Stan was, and vice versa. He almost lived at our house, and when he wasn't there, neither was Ada, and you knew that you'd find her at Stan's house. Luckily, he and his family lived not too far away. And he worked at the very firm that Ada worked for, which was, in the words of our mother, "a bit of luck."

And what was that firm? Grimwade's of Stoke. It was a pottery. Our town is known all over the world for the quality of the crockery the potteries make. Plates, cups, saucers, jugs, gravy boats . . . anything that belonged on a table or in a kitchen was the business of Grimwade's, and their factory spread itself over a large area very near where we lived. Many of the young men and women in our neighborhood ended up working there in some capacity. Stan's job was pushing trolleys piled high with plates from the kilns to the painting sheds. Ada was one of the painters. It was a good job, and when she was promoted from a wiper-up to an actual painter on the bench with the other women, Mam bought a joint of ham to celebrate. The money was good, and Ada liked the girls she worked with. She came home full of stories about Marge and Bessy and Sally and Phyllis and their doings and sayings. To hear her speak, usually when we were in our bed, whispering so as not to wake the Little Ones, days at Grimwade's passed in a whirl of funny tales told and jokes exchanged, with only the occasional bitter quarrel between the young women.

"But it's very hard work," Ada said, not wanting me to think she spent her days slacking off and having fun. "You don't dare stop, nor take your eyes off the piece you're on. You've got to get through the pile of plates. By the time I get off that stool, I'm seeing little flowers or ribbons or whatever I've been painting all over the place. Fussy work, it is."

I was the first person to know Ada was expecting. She'd not said a word to me, but one Sunday morning she jumped out of bed and ran out of our room and downstairs and out to the privy faster than I'd ever seen her. When she came back, she was as white as one of the unpainted plates she sometimes brought home from Grimwade's.

"What's the matter, Ada?" I asked. Often, in the winter, we

went out to the privy together, because it was a bit frightening out there in the dark.

"Sorry," she said, lying back down on the bed. "I couldn't wait for you. I felt . . . I felt ill."

I was just about to ask her whether she was fit enough to get up for breakfast when she burst into tears.

"What's the matter, Ada? Why are you crying?"

Ada never cried. I was the one who wept at everything. Ada was the happy one in the family.

"I'm going to have a baby," she said, turning her face into her pillow so that I had to strain to hear her.

"You'll have to tell Mam," I said. Ada groaned. I went on: "You have to. She'll find out soon enough."

Thoughts went chasing themselves around in my head. Stan still came to our house, but sometimes he'd call for Ada and they went for walks by themselves. There were days when they were gone for a long time, and when Ada returned, she'd tell me about how pretty the countryside looked and how much they'd enjoyed themselves.

I'd say, "I don't know where you find things to talk about with him for such a long time. I wouldn't know what to say."

And Ada would say, "Well, talking's not all we do."

I tried to imagine them kissing and holding hands, but it was hard. Stan was such an ordinary sort of young man, not particularly handsome, but with a bright and open smile.

It must be that she and Stan . . .

Would they now have to get married? Had she told him? She wasn't much of a writer, and he'd been in France since September. From time to time she got a postcard from him, and there was a small brownish photograph of Stan in uniform in a frame on the table on Ada's side of the bed. I read one of her postcards once. She'd left it on the table for a few moments. It didn't say much. *We are well and keeping cheerful as I hope you are too. Yours ever, Stan.*

"That's private, Maud," she'd said when she caught me reading it. She took it to hide away with all the other postcards, but as far as I could see, there was not a private word in it.

"He can't say anything proper," she explained to me. "He can't say he loves me. The captain or whoever it is who reads their letters would see it. He'd feel embarrassed, but I do so much want the words, Maudie. I mean, I know he *does* love me, but the words would be a comfort. Black on white would make the love . . . truer. A proper written fact."

I tried to comfort her when she spoke like that, telling her that Stan loved her whether he wrote down the words or not, but she still fretted, and in my heart I didn't blame her. I would have wanted the written words to look at as well.

I know Ada thought about Stan all the time and often wondered aloud what he'd be doing *just at that very moment.*

I thought of him too, and of all the other young men from around here who were out fighting against the Germans. I couldn't imagine what that was like.

Sometimes, you got a soldier coming home to one of the houses on our street, and everyone would go and wish them well and want to see them and hear what they had to say. The funny thing was, they didn't seem to want to talk much, any of them. One or two had limbs missing, and I couldn't even look at them like that. I'd keep my eyes on the floor when an amputee was in the room, and though I felt shame at my cowardice, I hated to think of the pain that they must have gone through. Hated to imagine how they must be feeling. Every single man who came back on leave from the fighting had black shadows under his eyes as if he hadn't slept since he'd left home.

I mentioned this to Mam one day at tea, and she sucked her cheeks in and said, "From what I hear, they're not sleeping much now that they're back, either. That's what Freda told me. It's the dreams. Nightmares, I should say." And she shook her head and poured herself another cup of tea from the pot on the table.

When Ada told our mother about her condition, Mam sank into the nearest chair and covered her face with her apron. Ada and I didn't know what to do. Mam was making strange noises, not quite crying and not quite sighing, and Ada said, sounding more scared than I'd ever heard her: "Mam?"

Mam gave one cry, as if she'd been wounded. Then she sniffed and said, "I'm all right." She took the apron off her head and smoothed it in her lap. "How far along are you?" she asked.

"I'm not quite sure. . . . Two months along, maybe."

Mam managed to calm down. "Well," she said, "I reckon Stan will marry you, unlike some. He's that fond of you. At least you won't be shamed by a baby no man wants to own . . . and if Stan dies over there . . ."

"Don't say that!" Ada cried. "How can you say such a thing to me?"

Mam put out a hand and patted Ada on the knee. "I'm sorry, pet, but you know that the men over there . . . well. It's to be expected. And we'll face it if we have to. I can say that the baby is my cousin Dora's, and I'm looking after the child because the father was killed in the war." She frowned. "You'll likely have to go up and stay with her for the birth, but we can worry about that when the time comes."

"I don't want to talk about it anymore," said Ada. "I want to stop feeling so ill, that's all."

She and Mam and I were downstairs by the kitchen fire. The Little Ones were in bed. The November darkness pressed against the windows, and we could hear the wind whistling in the chimney.

"But when is Stan's next leave due? We want you married as soon as possible."

"I don't know," Ada murmured. "I haven't told him yet."

"You have to tell him," I said.

"Plenty of time for that," said Mam. "No point getting his hopes up if she loses the child in the next few days."

"Mam!" I couldn't believe she was speaking like that and in front of Ada. It crossed my mind that she might think this would be an answer to all our problems, but then I dismissed that as unkind and unfair. Our mother was kind—the kindest possible mother.

"Don't you 'Mam' me!" she answered. "I've seen more babies miscarried than you've had hot dinners, so I'm not counting on anything yet." She turned to Ada again and said, "But if this baby hangs on, you'll feel better in another six weeks or so. I was just the same with all of you. Weak as a kitten and sick as sick for twelve weeks, and then right as a trivet for the rest of the time."

"But what can I do for the next six weeks?" Ada wailed. "I can't not work. We can't do without the money."

We sat in silence for a bit, and the fire waved its flames around and crackled, and we all thought about what could be done. Ada looked and sounded half dead. She could no sooner work than fly to the moon.

I said, "I know what to do. I know how we can manage."

"Can't be done," said Mam when I told her and Ada what I'd thought of doing.

"It can," said Ada. "I'll have to tell Phyllis and Betty, and they can tell the others on the line. No one will talk to the bosses."

"But Maudie doesn't look anything like you!" Mam said. "Who's going to be taken in for a minute?"

"If she wears my clothes, and keeps her mouth shut for most of the time, which won't be hard, considering the work we've got, what with the war on and the men being away. . . . You don't think the bosses actually *look* at us, do you? 'Cause they don't. One girl sitting at a bench with a paintbrush in her hand is much like another. She can go in with Phyllis. She'll show Maud what has to be done."

"But what if my work isn't as good as yours?" I asked Ada. "What if they notice that my flowers aren't so neat? What if I can't do what I'm supposed to do?"

"Course you'll be just as good as me. You're the neat one. You're Miss Portham's best pupil. . . ."

"Miss Portham!" I'd forgotten all about her. School had gone flying out of my head the moment I heard Ada's news. "What will I tell her?"

"I'll nip in to school and tell her you're ill. . . . That'll give us time to think," said Mam. "You're leaving at Christmas anyway, so there's not more than three weeks or so. . . ."

My eyes filled with tears at the thought that I might not be able to go back to school again. I'd always known that I was leaving, but I'd so looked forward to doing all the lovely Christmassy things for the last time. I nearly backed out then. Nearly said, *No, I can't do it. I'm scared.* If I got caught, Grimwade's might sack Ada, and then what would happen to us? Mam's wages weren't much, not to feed and clothe five of us. We needed Ada's wages.

"Right, then," said Mam. "No time to waste. Maudie, go and find Phyllis and tell her to bring Betty and come around here as soon as she can. Take your shawl. . . . It's cold out there."

I went to find Phyllis and told her about Ada and also all about my plan. She was a tall, redheaded girl with freckly skin and very long fingers. She wasn't pretty, but her pale-green eyes were like bottle glass, and she had the lads in the pottery after her like puppies following the smell of a roast dinner. That was what Ada used to say.

Phyllis told her mother she'd be back directly and came straight home with me.

"I knew Ada was going to have a baby before she did," she told me as we walked to Betty's house, our clogs making a clattering sound on the cobbles that lined the street. "Saw her not eating her lunch, and that was a sure sign, because Ada likes her food."

I nodded. Phyllis glanced at me and added, "I reckon we can get you to look enough like her to pass. Don't look so worried. What's the worst thing that can happen? No, don't answer that. . . . Still, there's worse things than that. Think of the poor lads out there getting shot. Any of them would change places with you, wouldn't they?"

I nodded. *Poor Stan,* I thought. *And poor Ada.* I heard her weeping in bed sometimes, especially when a postcard came and told her none of the things she really wanted to know.

I woke up early the next day: the day I had to be Ada for the first time. Ada had been awake even earlier, running to the privy to be sick. She lay on the bed and gave me instructions as I got dressed in her work clothes.

"Don't fold back the rim of your bonnet. Luckily, they're dead-set on our hair being covered at all times. Less chance of accidents, they say, and it's sweltering in the summer, but you'll be all right today. Keep your head down; look at your bench. There's a new job coming up today. Something special, Mr. Grimwade said. He sent down a note on Friday. Joe Ferris read it out to us . . . an honor, he said it was."

"What was? What's the special job?" My heart did a kind of lurch in my chest. Ada had explained her work to me as best she could, but a special job? Would I be able to do that?

"Don't worry—something about lettering. You know your letters, don't you?"

I nodded. I was good at my letters. My writing was good. Why did I need my lettering in a pottery factory? I'd been expecting flowers. I was quite good at flowers and leaves. Ever since Ada had gone to work at Grimwade's, I'd copied the patterns she'd shown me. I'd decorated all my exercise books at school with designs she'd helped me to perfect. We all had. Even Alfie was used to copying the patterns on our crockery. The pictures on the cups and saucers were the only pictures in the house, apart from the photograph of Stan in our bedroom and a postcard of my parents on their honeymoon, looking young and not like themselves.

Phyllis came to pick me up because it was my first day. "You'll be all right to find your own way, once you're used to it. I've spoken to the others on the bench. You'll be called 'Ada,' and that's who you'll be. Put a smile on—there's nowt to worry about, Maudie dear." She squeezed my hand, and I nearly cried because I was so grateful to her for her kindness.

I needn't have worried about anyone noticing I wasn't Ada. The pottery was in a state of turmoil. We all filed in and took our places on the bench. I kept my head down and my bonnet on and listened while Joe Ferris, the foreman, went over the work.

"It's a privilege!" He looked as excited as if he'd won a horse race. "Grimwade's has been chosen for this very special commission. We're making a butter dish that will be sold to make everyone aware of the importance of economizing on food now that those Germans are stopping our ships from bringing food into the country. Our pottery and no one else's has been chosen. And you're the ones, girls, who'll decorate the dishes. Since the war started, you've proved that you're the equals of any men. You're the best painters in Stoke, and these will be the best butter dishes in England."

"They won't be the *prettiest* butter dishes in the world," said Sally, who sat down next to me on my left. Phyllis was on my right.

For a moment, when I read the words that I was going to have to paint onto the pottery, I nearly fainted. There were so many of them. I had no idea where to begin. How to go on. Where were all those letters supposed to fit onto this small saucer-like dish?

SPECIAL MESSAGE FROM
THE RT HON, D. LLOYD GEORGE, PRIME MINISTER

"I HAVE NO HESITATION IN SAYING THAT ECONOMY IN THE CONSUMPTION
& USE OF FOOD IN THIS COUNTRY IS A MATTER OF THE GREATEST POSSIBLE
IMPORTANCE TO THE EMPIRE AT THE PRESENT TIME."

That was on the front, and there was still more on the back:

THE WAR TIME BUTTER DISH FOR A FAMILY OF TEN.
MADE BY THE GIRLS OF STAFFORDSHIRE DURING THE WINTER OF 1917
WHEN THE BOYS WERE IN THE TRENCHES FIGHTING
FOR LIBERTY AND CIVILIZATION.

And then there was the border . . . little laurel leaves all the way around the edge of the dish.

"Copy me," said Phyllis. "Watch what I do, and do the same. Look, they've given us the specimen on this sheet of paper. That's how it's to be laid out. . . . Best make a start."

Once I'd started, once I had dipped my thin brush in the heavy paint and pretended it was a funny kind of pen, things were better. I forgot about being frightened, but oh, how long it took! I hadn't even finished two butter dishes by the time it came to unpacking my lunch and eating it with the others on a bench in the packing room. Everyone gathered around me. Clearly, word about Ada had gotten out, and the women wanted to know how she was and promised to help and cover for me with the bosses if they needed to. By the time I went back to my bench, I was one of them: one of the workers. And by the time I walked home with Phyllis, I was so tired I could have lain down on the pavement and fallen asleep right there in the midst of everyone making their way back through the twilight.

There was no going straight to bed, either. Ada wanted to know everything. What I'd done, what the women had said about her.

"What about Mardy Molly? Didn't she say I was no better than I should be and this was God's punishment?"

"I never met Mardy Molly," I told her. "And if she'd said that to me, I'd have given her a piece of my mind!"

"Ooh, I'd love to have a look at that dish. It sounds like a great deal too many letters to go on such a small space."

"Well, it didn't look too bad once the words were there. Not as pretty as a proper pattern, of course, but not too bad."

When I went to bed, I found I was looking forward to the next day. To be working at something I was good at and for which I was being paid real money that we could spend. The rest of my family would be fed and clothed because of my work and not the other way around, with me being fed and clothed from the efforts of my mother and my sister. That made me feel powerful. It made me think, *I can do this even after Ada's all right again. I can go to Grimwade's on my own account. I can be a craftsperson, if I have a gift for it. I can have a job for the rest of my life if I want one.* The letters on the back of the dish danced in front of my eyes when I closed them. I wouldn't have to look at the paper tomorrow.

I knew the words by heart: *Made by the girls of Staffordshire during the winter of 1917 when the boys were in the trenches fighting for liberty and civilization.*

Stan was the last thing I thought about before I fell asleep. Poor Stan over there in France being shot at and lying in mud and not having enough to eat of anything, much less butter. I felt fortunate.

I pretended to be Ada for another six weeks. Every day at the pottery I worried about being found out, but Phyllis and the others made sure I was kept away from the managers and the owners. Sometimes men came to inspect our work, but mine never caused any comment.

"You're good at this," Phyllis said. "When Ada comes back, come and see about a job here. Tell them Ada's been teaching you at home. They like having workers from the same families." And that is what I did.

Stan survived the Great War, though he'd been wounded: he had a scarred cheek, as though the skin had been melted and reformed in a series of ridges and bumps. He came home just after Christmas, and he and Ada were married shortly afterward. The baby was a girl, and they called her Maud after me, which was lovely.

On my birthday in the spring of 1918, I opened a present from Stan and Ada, and there it was: one of the special butter dishes. They had bought it for me, to remind me of the first paid work I'd ever done. I knew it was one of the ones I'd made because I recognized my own handwriting.

"Let's have a closer look at it," said Ada.

I gave it to her, and she turned it around in her hands.

"Look, there's a bit of a blotch here. . . . Can you see?"

Ada peered at the mark I'd shown her. "Well, it was only your first job," she said. "Now that you're working at Grimwade's yourself, you'll soon be doing much more complicated patterns."

I've kept the dish for years. I hope that my children and my grandchildren will still spread butter from it onto their toast every day, long after I'm gone.

Previous page: **WOMEN WELDING**
Before 1914, most women worked only in traditionally female jobs such as teaching and domestic service. But when war broke out, women were needed to take over for men in factory, transportation, and farm jobs. Public perceptions of women changed, and many countries, including Britain and the United States, introduced votes for women soon after the war.

Captain Rosalie

TIMOTHÉE DE FOMBELLE

TRANSLATED BY SAM GORDON

I have a secret.

The others think I am drawing in my notebook when I am sitting on the little bench underneath the coat pegs at the back of the class. They think I am dreaming as I wait for evening to fall. And the teacher passes me by as he gives dictation to the students.

He places his hand on my hair.

But I am a soldier on a mission. I am spying on the enemy.

I am preparing my plan.

Captain Rosalie.

I am disguised as a little girl, five and a half years old, with my shoes, my dress, and my red hair. To let me go unnoticed, I do not wear a helmet or a uniform. I stay there, silent. To the older children, I am the little girl who comes and sits at the back of the class and does nothing all day long.

My mother has worked at the factory since the start of the war, ever since my father went to fight. Now I am too old to go to the nanny's, so every morning I am dropped beneath the sheltered part of the yard at the school for the older children, before the sun is even up.

The courtyard is deserted. I wait all by myself, eating the bread and butter that my mother has knotted into one of my father's big handkerchiefs. Dogs bark in the distance, out there by the farms. The dead leaves whistle their way across the courtyard.

The teacher arrives at seven o'clock in the morning. Since coming back from the war, he has only had one arm. But he smiles as though having one is already quite a thing. That and being here in the silence of the school.

"Still at your post, young lady?"

He should be calling me "Captain" and clicking his heels, but I keep quiet. Secret mission. I must not give anything away.

The teacher said to my mother at the start of the year that he would look after me, that he would let me sit at the back of the older children's class and do my drawing, that he would give me a notebook and some pencils. My mother shook his hand for a very long time to show her thanks.

I hold his large bag in my lap while he opens up the school. His belongings have an aroma of wood smoke and coffee. This must be what it smells like in his brightly lit house just behind the school.

One of the older children, Edgar, always arrives before the others, because he is in trouble and has to light the stove in the classroom as punishment. I like Edgar a lot. I can see that he does not listen to a thing, that he refuses to learn how to count or read, but one day I will make him a lieutenant. Edgar lets me strike the match before throwing it into the stove. The fire, when it gets going, is the same color as my hair, like a little brother who looks like me.

When the students arrive, I am already sitting down at the back of the class in my place against the wall. They are two or three years older than I am. I let myself be covered by the coats as they hang them above my head without paying any attention to me. I wait a bit, and when they are all at their desks with their backs to me, I push the coats aside as if I were bursting from a bush and taking their patrol from behind in a clearing.

Only Edgar notices me, with my notebook gripped in my hand.

But I am already listening to the teacher, who is reading

aloud the first page of the newspaper. Every morning he gives news of the war.

"Yesterday, Tuesday, the German troops were crushed at the Somme. Our men are fighting and reporting victories." Then he says, "We must have faith."

And then some mysterious names: Combles, Thiepval . . . recaptured villages.

The teacher always gives us good news, never bad. He leaves the students standing behind their chairs a little longer, in silence. He tells them that they must think of our soldiers who are giving up their youth, their life. Sometimes, when he speaks like that, I get the feeling that he is looking at me, and I turn away so as not to catch his eye. How could he know about my mission? When at last the class sits down, I pretend to be elsewhere, lost in my thoughts, even though I am concentrating perfectly. I am Captain Rosalie, and I have infiltrated their squad this fall morning in 1917. I know what I must do. One day I will be awarded a medal for this. It is already gleaming deep within me.

The freckles beneath my eyes, the animals I draw on the page, the long socks up to my knees . . . all that is just camouflage. I have heard that soldiers hide with bracken sewn into their uniforms. My ferns are the scabs on my legs, the vacant daydreaming, the tunes I hum—a sweet little melody for a sweet little lady.

The teacher marks out symbols on the blackboard, and the students recite them. I watch the boy in the first row as he stands up and approaches the board to write some other mystical signs. He never makes a mistake. His name is Robert, the gendarme's son. The teacher congratulates him and sends him back to his place. I keep a close eye on Robert. I know the importance of being able to recognize the best soldiers and pinching their secrets.

The teacher whispers as he passes close by me.

"Go and get some coal, Rosalie. That'll keep you occupied."

I stand up from my bench. The coal is stored outside, behind the classroom, beneath the window. I must not show that I do not want to be away.

"You can leave your book."

But I keep it in my hand. Never let the enemy seize your weapons. As soon as I reach the door, I run through the cold toward the pile of coal. I have to get back very quickly. I must not abandon my post.

In the evenings, my mother comes to pick me up from the empty school. The teacher and the students have long since left. She squeezes me in her arms and rubs her head against mine. Lucky I'm not wearing my helmet. I breathe in the scent of her hair, which smells good.

"I've missed you, Rosalie."

She is very tired, and I love this tiredness. I love it when courage deserts her and her eyes are red. But very quickly she composes herself and takes my hand.

"Look!"

She brings an envelope out of her pocket. I recognize these white envelopes, covered in postmarks and black and red stamps. It is a letter from my father.

"Come, Rosalie. I'll read it to you."

As she pulls me along by my hand, no one can see anything on my face. I show nothing of my thoughts. I feel my mother's fingers clinging hard to my ink-stained hand.

"When I get home, I'm going to take Rosalie fishing."

Lying on my bed, I look at my mother from the side, the letter perched in her lap.

"I thought about the stream below the mill. I saw some trout leaping there before the war. Rosalie will learn to swim. Do you have that recipe for trout with walnuts? Can you be sure that there are some walnuts left for it if I come home in the spring?"

I close my eyes. I don't like all this stuff. My mother continues.

*"My darling, I am thinking of you. I know that Rosalie
is a good girl. And that the teacher is happy to have her and
help her. And as for you, I know your work is tiring. You'd
like to spend more time with your little girl. But every time
I load a shell into the cannon, I say to myself that maybe
it was you who made it at the factory. It's like you are at
my side in battle. Yes, the ladies are helping us by working
so hard in the factories, and the children keep us going by
lending their mothers support and being good."*

I try not to listen. Anyway, I could not care less about being
good. I do not lend my mother to anyone. I do not want to hear
any talk of fish leaping in streams. I do not believe in stories of
walnuts and mills.

Not one memory other than war. I was too young before it.
And I can see that my mother is still reading, for a long time,
although there is just a single page of writing in the envelope. I
can see that she continues even when the candle stops flickering
in the bedroom.

She shows me a drawing on the back of the sheet of paper,
lines of charcoal depicting a landscape. It's the only thing that
seems true. A forest in the distance and the land in the fore-
ground all churned up, with soldiers hiding in holes. I can tell
my father's way of drawing. I have seen him three times when

he has been home on leave to have a rest from the war. He hardly spoke, but he held me tight in his arms and he drew horses in the mist on the window.

I fall asleep thinking of horses streaming across the glass.

In bed, I dream of a medal being attached to my nightdress. I dream of a general placing his hand on my shoulder. I feel the coldness of the medal against my skin.

Each day, my mission continues its advance. Each day, I, Captain Rosalie, am at my post at the back of the class, waiting in ambush beneath the coats.

I look at the inscriptions on the blackboard as if they form a battle plan. I try to remember everything. I copy little bits down in the back pages of my notebook. No one pays me any attention. The older children have forgotten about me. I have become a gray coat hooked amid the others. Only the teacher remembers me from time to time. And Edgar, the dunce, my lieutenant, who throws curious looks my way. I feel he is waiting for his time to come.

In the evening, my mother comes to collect me. Sometimes she has a new letter in her pocket, sometimes not. Just that beckoning to take me into her arms, those eyes that never leave mine. I prefer this to all that talk about the trout we are going to fish for, about swimming in the stream or the jams we will make one day after picking wild raspberries. The letters stay in the toffee box, on top of the shelves in the kitchen. Better up there.

The weeks are very alike. From time to time at night, I open my window and lean out to listen. To listen carefully. I wonder if I might hear the noise of the war, way off in the distance, beyond the dogs at the farms.

And then one day, on my birthday, I am given snow. Snow up to above my ankles. I can barely open the door when I wake up. I let out a cry. Flakes are falling all around.

My mother does not go to the factory that day because it is snowing too heavily. I stay with her at home. This must be the greatest day of my life. We play hide-and-seek in the house. She does not even get dressed. I find her curled up in bed, still wearing her nightgown. She startles me. I forget about Captain Rosalie. I almost forget about my father. My mother rolls me up in a blanket, laughing. Since there is nothing to eat and we cannot go out, we drink milk sweetened with sugar. We cuddle together in the same armchair opposite the fireplace. I watch the redheaded flames as they dance. Then she climbs up to fetch the big cloth on top of the wardrobe. She brings out her wedding dress. She shows me that it still fits her.

"It's just a little tight here — look."

She laughs again. Before nightfall, dressed in white, she tells me a true story with desert islands and princesses.

But later, in my sleep, I hear a knock on the windowpane. I hear someone speaking to my mother in the next room. I do not manage to wake up. It's a man who has come to see her to tell her something. I recognize the voice of the gendarme. My eyes stay screwed shut. And then I hear a cry. A cry that is very long and very low, a cry that is partly stifled. But I cannot tell whether I am dreaming or if it is real.

The following day, it is clear that nothing will ever be like before. There is a blue envelope in the kitchen. It is impossible to meet my mother's eye. She retreats when I go near her. She talks quickly, lowering her head. I already have my wool bonnet and my coat. I look at her. She is fretting, as if she were late, yet she does nothing. She picks up the envelope as she passes and makes it disappear. She rolls the wedding dress into a ball and stuffs it on top of the wardrobe. She offers me her hand and takes me outside, her face hidden in her shawl. The snow is already melting. It will be muddy in the schoolyard.

For a month I have lived in the memory of that night after the snow. My mother still cannot bring herself to look at me. She has changed. When she drops me at school in the morning, I find it almost comforting when she goes. She walks off, shuffling, even though the ground is no longer at all slippery.

I must act quickly. *We're counting on you, Captain.* I prepare everything so that I will be ready when my day comes.

And finally that day does come.

It is a sunny morning in February.

At the back of the class, I make every effort to follow the chalk across the blackboard. Nothing gets past me. Every movement of the teacher's hand. He turns around, shaking the white dust from his sleeve.

I look afresh at the board. For the first time, it all becomes clear. As if a fog has suddenly lifted, making everything appear. My mission is nearly complete.

I must not wait any longer. This is the moment. I am ready. I think of the medal I saw in my dream. It all becomes possible. Now I must fight out in the open.

"Young lady?"

The teacher is in front of me. I had not even realized that my hand was raised to call him. It's the first time. I've never asked anything until now.

I explain that I have forgotten my notebook at home. I want to go get it. The teacher says that's not possible.

I look at him seriously. I sit up very straight, my eyes trained on him.

"It's just at the end of the road. I know the way."

"You can take a sheet of paper."

"I need my notebook."

"No. You are staying here."

His tone is final.

I bring out my second weapon before he has time to turn away. My gaze suddenly drops to my shoes. And there is already a tear forming between my eyelashes.

This time, the blow appears to find its target. Panic in the enemy ranks. The lines cannot hold for much longer when faced with a crying little girl. But I need reinforcements.

A voice rings out just beside me.

"I can go with her."

It's Edgar. He seems so well behaved that I do not recognize him.

The teacher wavers. I wipe away my tears with my fist. He nervously rubs his hand, still covered in chalk, on the pocket of his overgarment.

"Very well."

He looks at me. Then at Edgar. Then back at me.

"You have ten minutes. I don't like it when students take off like this."

I walk down the street with my lieutenant behind me. The village is deserted. Wet rooftops shine beneath a cold sun. Smoke drifts from the chimney of the bakery. What is there to show that a war is going on? The fighting is so far from us. There are birds playing around the church's bell tower. I see them skimming past the chimes.

Our patrol arrives in front of the house.

"Here we are."

"Is it open?" Edgar asks.

I take the key from where it is hidden in the lizard's hole, to the left of the door. I'm not even scared of the lizard. I hand the key to Edgar.

"Open it, please."

The lock is old. Usually the key doesn't turn. But Edgar opens the door easily. I point to the large stone for him to sit on.

"Wait for me. I won't be long."

He crouches next to the stone. He's my best soldier.

When I enter the house, I feel as though in that one instant I have grown up. I have never been in here by myself. I take a first step. There are only two rooms: my bedroom, which used to be my parents' when I was much younger, and the kitchen. That's where my mother has slept since the war.

I push the kitchen door. I feel as though all the objects are looking at me. Even the clock is wondering what I am doing there.

But still I pull a chair toward the shelves. It groans against the floor to tell me it does not agree. I climb up and take hold of the metal box, right there at the top. I look at it in my hands.

And the miracle happens. The box speaks to me. I have seen it so often, sitting there mute on the table, with its drawings of sheep resting beneath a tree, the shepherd in the distance . . . This closed box starts talking. The words come slowly.

Assorted . . . candies.

It's written there, on one line, in violet letters.

I have been fighting that for months. It was my mission. I can read.

I get down from my chair, place the box on the table, and push open the lid. The envelopes are there.

I take the one on top. I open it. I am too breathless to follow my father's sloping handwriting, but I pick out the smallest words, those that jump toward my face as I lean over.

The word *rats,* the word *blood,* the word *fear.*

My mother never read me those words.

There's an underlined sentence that says, *The rain here is made of metal and fire.*

And lower down, as if they had collapsed to the foot of the page, the words *buried alive* and *butchery.*

I look for the letter where he had drawn the soldiers at the edge of the forest. Here it is. I unfold it. I look for the word *trout* and the word *stream* that my mother had read out. There is no sign of any stream, any trout, any mill. Nothing.

All that is written is *At night I cry in the mud* and *Oh, my darling, you will never see me again.*

At the end I see my name. He wrote it in lovely round letters, as if it were in a different language, as if I were from a different planet.

Give Rosalie a kiss.

"What are you doing?" Edgar's voice. I do not turn around. He must not see his captain's tears.

"You can read?" he asks.

I jam the letters back into the box. My hands are shaking. I am looking for the blue envelope.

"Did you learn to read?" he says again.

"I want to find my notebook."

"You hid it under your shirt. You already had it in the classroom. We have to go. They'll find us."

I put the box back on the shelf. I pull out the notebook that was tucked under my shirt.

I imagine metal falling from the sky, my father lying beneath the burning rain.

As we leave the house, I feel pain, but something has opened inside me. I stop a second. I breathe in the pure, pungent air of truth.

"Why didn't you tell the teacher that I had the notebook beneath my shirt?" I ask Edgar on the way back.

He shrugs and continues walking ahead of me.

"Because we're on the same side."

I am back on my bench in the classroom. I am thinking about the blue envelope. Where has it gone? It arrived the night after the snow. It knows the final secret. There have been no letters since.

I no longer listen in on everything around me.

It's the end of the morning. Lunchtime. Thinking back, I don't remember the hours that followed.

When the bell rings for recess, everyone rushes to grab their coats. I stay there, sitting through the storm. "Are you coming?" I hear Edgar ask. I do not move. Some of the students start to go out to the courtyard.

"If they come looking for me," I say to Edgar, "tell them I went to the stream, up by the mill."

He looks at me. The commotion continues around us.

"Do you need me?"

"I need you to tell them that I went to the stream. Okay?"

He stands down.

I slip off the bench and curl into a ball. The teacher stamps his foot at the door.

"Get a move on! Outside."

He is already stuffing his pipe with tobacco.

"Edgar!" he yells. "I'm about to shut the door."

Edgar files out. I stay hidden under my bench. The door slams.

I can hear my breathing in the deserted room. After a few seconds, I slide toward the window, the one that faces the street.

I open it. I hesitate a moment. The sweet smell of the pipe is coming around from the yard, along with the cries of the children.

Finally I scale the window and jump out onto the street. I don't take the direction of the stream. I run home.

I grab the key from the lizard's hole. For the first time, I manage to open the door. The box. The letters spread across the kitchen table. The blue envelope is not there. I stand up.

I look in the saucepans, in the drawers, in the cabinet by the entrance, in the wardrobe. I search the pockets of my mother's clothes and among the papers in the big red file. Where is the letter? I no longer know what I am doing. I look under the mattress, between the slats of the bed. I completely unmake my mother's bed. The sheets lie strewn around the room like ghosts.

And then, suddenly, I look up to the top of the wardrobe. The wedding dress, rolled up in a bundle. I climb onto the stove just next to it. I lift up the dusty robe. I cannot see a thing as I run my hand underneath.

It's there. Under the lace of the veil. I take the square blue envelope.

I go and sit down at the table. I open it.

Ministry of War.

These three words written at the top. I only read the ones that come to me.

Madame, regret, pain, and then my father's full name. And

then seven more words that feel like seven cannon shots in the early evening.

Killed in action fighting for his country.

These words resound in me long into the night. They kick up a cloud of dust.

Killed in action fighting for his country.

As for the rest, Edgar told me sometime later.

Class resumes after recess, and it takes the teacher a moment to notice my absence. Not much different from the sense that a piece of furniture is missing from the room.

"And the little one?"

He inspects the coat pegs, walks between the rows of desks, and makes the pupils stand up as if one of them might have sat on me or hidden me in his pocket. He looks under his desk.

"Sir, Edgar wants to say something."

And indeed Edgar is there with his hand up.

The teacher goes over to him.

"She told me something about the stream. She told me she wanted to go to the stream by the mill."

"The stream."

The teacher spins around, his face white. He seems to be searching for an escape route.

"My God, the stream. Put on your coats."

In an instant, everyone is outside. This might have been

cause for excitement, but a deep silence reigns. The only sound is the hammering of soles across the school yard.

The teacher turns to Robert, the gendarme's son.

"You, go and find your father."

The pupils set off on the double toward the stream. It's the first time anyone has seen the teacher run. Darkness starts to fall. Edgar leads the troops.

When they get to the bank, they see that the water has risen. The stream is a torrent. The teacher is so pale, he looks like a worm glistening in the shadow of the willows.

"My God!" he murmurs. "What drove her to this?"

Edgar organizes two parties. One to go upstream, the other down. The gendarme arrives with his son and another policeman. They go and investigate the wheel of the mill, which is striving to keep up with everything the current sends its way.

"What about her mother?" asks the teacher. "What do we tell her mother?"

A sputtering of voices can be heard here and there along the water.

"Rosalie! Rosalie!"

"Can she swim?"

"Rosalie!"

And everyone realizes they have never uttered my first name.

It is pitch-black when my mother arrives. She stops by the

school, where a student is keeping watch. He tells her that I have disappeared. She runs to the stream.

The teacher goes to meet her. He has mud on his nose and in his hair. His shoes are filled with water.

"Madame . . ."

He is incapable of saying anything more. My mother looks at the surface of the water. The gendarme has returned from the mill.

"She spoke of this place to a fellow student. Did your daughter sometimes come up here?"

My mother does not answer. The gendarme takes her by the arm and draws her to one side.

"Tell me . . . is there any way that the news of her father . . . ?"

"No," says my mother, her voice weak.

"She seemed so strong. . . ."

"I didn't tell her anything about her father."

"Sorry?"

"I haven't been able to tell her. I can't. Every evening, I try to talk to her, but . . ."

She looks away.

The gendarme falls silent.

Edgar steps out of the shadows. He has heard everything.

"I just wanted to say, I think I saw Rosalie at your house through the kitchen window. The door is locked from the inside."

Now there are fifty people outside the house, waiting in the darkness. My mother goes up to the window. She presses herself against the glass.

"Rosalie . . ." It's all my mother can say.

She sees me asleep amid the letters, my head on the table. The wax from the candle is melting onto the envelopes next to me.

"What's all that around her?" asks the teacher, whose forehead is resting on the windowpane.

"She can read," says Edgar, swelling with pride.

The teacher turns to him, lost.

"What did you say?"

"She can read, sir!"

"My God," he gasps.

A dull sound. The gendarme has just forced the door. He does not want to be the first to go in. He calls out to my mother.

She leaves the window, moving toward him.

The students form a guard of honor to make way for her.

She enters, alone, slowly.

I open my eyes. The flame of the candle makes the kitchen look like it has been painted gold.

I see my mother.

I sit up straight in my chair.

Her face is how I like it. Like it is on the difficult days.

She stays on her feet, by the table.

"I wanted to know," I say to her.

"Yes, Rosalie."

"And now I do."

"Yes."

She steps forward, takes me in her arms, and I cry with her.

The gendarme disperses the little crowd by the entrance. Bright dots vanish into the night.

My mother takes a blue envelope from her pocket. It is thicker, a package that says *Ministry of War* and that she has already opened.

"I received this today. It's for you."

I open the parcel. First of all there is a letter. I make out the words *Died for his country* that I already know. And then some other incomprehensible words, *posthumously* and *grateful compatriots*. But inside the package, underneath the letter, sits a heavy object in a little velvet bag.

I turn toward the window.

Edgar is outside, looking at me. I smile at him through my tears.

"It's for you," says my mother again.

I open the bag on the table.

It's a medal made of sparkling bronze with blue trimming.

Like a little fish, alive in my hands.

Previous page: **THE WRECKAGE OF WAR**
Heavy fighting left villages and towns in ruins, including the ancient Belgian town of Ypres, and permanently changed the face of the French and Belgian countryside. After the war, Germany was forced to pay the Allies substantial reparations, which were used to rebuild places that had been destroyed.

SHEENA WILKINSON

EACH WILKINSON

SLOW DUSK

The school flag is at half-mast. Again.

As I drag myself up the driveway, I see Maud waiting at the top of the steps.

"Edith!" she shrieks, in the way that always makes Miss Thomas shake her head and remind her that a lady is known by her gentle voice. I try to hurry, but the steps feel steeper than usual and my skirt heavier. I can't believe it's only Wednesday; time seems to have slowed down since Gilbert came home.

"You needn't have waited." I pause at the top of the steps to catch my breath. "You don't want a late mark on my account."

"I don't want to go in to prayers alone," she says, frowning in a very un-Maudlike way.

"It may not be anyone we know." I tuck my arm into Maud's, and we set out toward the chapel. "Last time it wasn't even anything to do with the war—it was that old matron from a million years ago."

"And at least your Gilbert's safe and sound now."

"*Safe*," I say. "Not exactly *sound*. They don't invalid you out of the army for nothing."

"Yes, but *rheumatism*. It's not as if he's lost a limb or—"

"It's very debilitating. There are days—nights especially—" But I don't want to talk about this. Instead I say, and I feel like a beast as soon as the words are out, "And *obviously* it's not Frank."

Maud yanks her arm away and stomps ahead. Even her swinging dark braid looks offended.

Miss Cassidy is at the chapel door, hurrying people along. "Come on, Edith! Not like you to be late." She gives me a quizzical glance.

The organ is playing softly. Sun slants through the stained-glass windows and plays on the wooden floor. The usual morning muttering has something uneasy about it. I slip into a place at the back beside Sally Craig just as the headmaster,

Dr. Allen, steps forward to the lectern and announces Hymn 341: "O God, Our Help in Ages Past."

"Who is it?" I whisper to Sally. She shrugs. I wish I hadn't said anything to Maud about Frank. I'm usually the one to stick up for him when she complains about him not joining up.

As if the flag and that particular hymn were not clues enough, when Dr. Allen comes back to the lectern after the hymn, his face is stern and his voice toneless.

"It is my painful duty to have to tell you that we have lost yet another Old Boy," he says. I grimace at Sally. *Please let it be someone we don't know, someone who left ten years ago, or twenty.* "And a boy known to all of you in this room, except the new pupils, for he left school only last June to join the Royal Irish Rifles as a cadet. Piers McBride was killed in action three days ago near Messines. Piers was one of our finest young men . . ."

Piers McBride. Nobody makes a sound—gasping is frowned on—but I can *feel* everyone gasp inside.

Dr. Allen continues. "Piers has been very much a part of our community since kindergarten. He was a brilliant sportsman — we all remember the cup-winning rugby team of 1914: Piers played a vital role in that victory despite being the youngest player by some two years."

He was pals with Gilbert. I remember him coming to tea. I was too shy to talk to him, but he was quite jolly, got down on the hearth rug and played with the kittens. Mother said he was a tonic and he must come again. Maud and I packed an Old Boys' Cake Fund package for him only last week.

"Piers was an only son," Dr. Allen goes on. "His sister, Patricia, is one of our prefects. I need hardly tell you that when she returns to school, you must all be very understanding."

Tears prick the backs of my eyes, and I blink in annoyance at myself. After all, we are used to this kind of news by now. And Piers must have *wanted* to go—he could have waited until he was old enough for a commission, but he was worried the war might be over before he had his chance.

I don't think it will ever be over.

We are all silent marching out of prayers to first class. I risk a smile at Maud as we file into the chalk-smelling Latin room, and she smiles back and sits in her usual seat beside me.

I like Latin but not with old Mullan, who is about ninety-three and was quietly festering until he came out of retirement to replace one of the younger masters who joined up. He never calls on the girls, so I busy myself writing a list of books inside the back cover of my exercise book. Miss Cassidy says I should start reading seriously now: if I want a university entrance scholarship, I can't rely on just studying the matriculation curriculum.

"And is there any chance of your being able to go to Queen's without a scholarship?" she had asked tactfully. There might have been, once, but Mother's illness cost a good deal. The fear that has started to rear its head since Mother died flashes into my head — *You can't go to college now. Everything is different* — but I squash it and imagine the wrought-iron gates of Queen's University swinging open to let me in. Not just to study. To a whole glittering future. Dickens. We have all his novels in the bookcase in the parlor. The Brontës. I've read *Jane Eyre*. It was —

"Miss Hamilton?" Mr. Mullan's voice blares. "Do I have your full attention? Clearly not. Thinking of hats, hmmm? Or frocks? One of the boys, then. McVicker?"

James McVicker swaggers to the board. I will him to make a mistake, but he doesn't. Maud scrawls on the corner of her scribbler: *OBCF at break?*

I nod, but don't give Mullan the satisfaction of seeing me. I stare at the blackboard and try not to yawn. I wonder how Gilbert is now. Father says it's early days, and he is still recovering from the rough crossing from Liverpool and the journey from France before that, and the weeks in hospital. And the fighting before that. He was trapped in a shell hole all night after an attack with two others, up to his waist in freezing water. He knew he was supposed to leave them, but he wouldn't, and after a few hours, his limbs were so seized up that he couldn't, even though his companions were now dead. Father says he will be his old self in no time.

Maud's in the storeroom before me, unpacking boxes and laying things out on the big central table. This is the hub of operations for the Old Boys' Cake Fund. There are no windows, and it gets hot from the boiler room next door, and the dust makes people sneeze, so enthusiasm for the OBCF has waned. When we first thought of making up packages to send to Old Boys at the front in time for Christmas 1914, all the girls and lots of the boys were mad about it, but now only a few stalwarts do the actual packing and sorting, though the stream of cakes and cigarettes and socks and sweets is steady enough.

Maud holds up what look like two deformed wooly eels. "We can't send *these* to the front, can we?"

We collapse giggling over the socks, and when Miss Thomas comes in, she frowns. "I wouldn't have thought this was a day for giggling, girls. I'd have expected better from *you*, Edith Hamilton."

Maud mutters something, setting the socks down on the table and untying the string on a cake box. Miss Thomas glares at her, but she's chronically short of volunteers, and Maud is a tireless worker for the OBCF.

Maud systematically fills boxes — one cake, one bag of sweets, one box of cigarettes, one knitted item — though she hides the deformed socks in some discarded packaging. "Maybe the juniors could try scarves instead," she suggests.

"Are there any letters this week?" I ask Miss Thomas. It's my job to select extracts from the Old Boys' letters and give them to the editor of the school magazine. At the start of the war, Old Boys used to send articles about life at the front, but there hasn't been one of those since the Somme.

"Two." Miss Thomas reaches into her attaché case and hands me two small envelopes. "I haven't had a chance to open them yet."

I slit open the first envelope. It's from someone I've never heard of, who left years ago—he's a doctor with the Royal Army Medical Corps, and he says it was wonderful to be remembered by his old school. *What a splendid plum cake. I was quite the most popular chap in the place!*

I smile and pass it to Maud and open the next one. It's the usual thing, in a bold, untidy hand: *I remember bringing in cakes and sweets for the Old Boys myself not so long ago. How jolly to be on the receiving end! We've had a sticky time the last few days, so your parcel gave me and my pals quite a "lift." And what splendid socks. We spend a lot of time on our feet here, and cozy socks like these are just the ticket. Do remember me to the dear old school and tell the rugby team not to be slacking! Piers McBride.*

My hand flies to my mouth, and I can't help the little gasp that escapes.

"What?" Maud finishes tying up a package and frowns at me. I hand her over the sheet of paper.

As soon as she reads it, she gives a choked sob and sits down heavily. "What is it *now*, Maud?" Miss Thomas asks.

"It's from Piers," I say.

Miss Thomas's face softens. "Oh, dear. How distressing. I wonder—I expect his parents would like to have it. It may be the last one. Piers was always happier with a ball than a pen. . . ." She holds her hand out for the letter, and Maud, after a slight hesitation, gives it to her. Miss Thomas slots the single sheet of paper carefully into its envelope. "Edith, can I trust you to give it to Patricia when she returns to us, or would you rather the staff handled it?"

Maud and I exchange glances. "I'll take it," I say.

"Go and get some fresh air, girls, before break's over," Miss Thomas says. "I'll take over here."

I link arms with Maud on the way out to the grounds. "Old Thomas sounded quite *human* for once," I say.

"*I* knitted those socks."

"The *deformed* ones?"

"*Piers's* socks. I knitted the loveliest socks you've ever seen, and I made sure they went into *his* parcel because—well, because." She chews her lip. "I wonder if he was wearing them when—"

"Stop it, Maud. You're being morbid."

She sighs. "I *hate* knitting. I want to do something . . . important." She pulls away from me and spreads her arms wide, raising her face to the weak March sun that's struggling through the trees at the edge of the cricket pitch. I shrug myself into my blazer. "The war's going to end, and I won't have had a chance to do *anything*."

"Socks *are* important. Even Piers said so. And the rotten war might *never* end."

"I want to go out there. Lots of girls do. I could be a nurse or drive an ambulance or . . ."

"Not at sixteen. Anyway, you can still be a nurse after the war."

"Oh, no. I hate sick people. I'd only want to nurse *soldiers*. Not old men and mewling brats."

When Maud goes on like this, I often wonder if her ambition to do something in the war is because Frank won't.

"Well, women can be almost anything they want nowadays. That's one thing the war has changed for the better."

"You sound like Miss Cassidy. Anyway, I'm not brainy like you. Wanting to go to college. No fear." Maud wrinkles her nose. "My cousin went to Somerville, and my aunt says she's *ruined* her marriage prospects. And Jessie said it was stricter than school."

"Don't talk about it." I make myself concentrate on my dream of the gates. Open and welcoming.

"I thought you *loved* talking about it. I thought you couldn't wait."

I shake my head. If I don't speak the fear aloud, maybe it will go away.

The class before lunch is my favorite—English with Miss Cassidy. *Othello.* I'm Desdemona, which would be lovely if my Othello weren't James McVicker. Most of the boys in the upper fifth are so *puerile*—though they could be leading soldiers into battle in two years if the war is still on.

After class, Miss Cassidy keeps me back. "Is everything all right, Edith?" she asks. "You seem—distracted. And you didn't come for your scholarship coaching yesterday."

"I'm sorry. I—well, I forgot."

"That's not like you. Nor is coming to school late." It's a question rather than a statement.

"My brother's home from the hospital."

"But that's good, isn't it? You must be pleased that he's out of danger now, and nobody can say he hasn't done his bit."

"Yes. But there's a lot to do. He's not quite well yet."

"But you have a nurse?"

I shake my head. Not even to Miss Cassidy can I admit that Father says we can't afford a nurse. "And what do we need one for, when we have you?" is what he'd said when I broached the subject before Gilbert came home. "It's not as if Gilbert has any wounds to be dressed. He's just got"—he recited the diagnosis we both knew by heart—"general debility caused by exposure.

Rheumatism. Heart and lungs not quite the thing." He managed to make it sound very trifling.

"It's hard for him to adjust after being in the hospital for so long. I think he's lonely. All of his friends are away at war." Or dead. Except Frank, of course, but Frank hasn't called.

"But you *must* find time for your studies! Your future—"

I sigh. Does she really think I don't *want* to study?

"I'll try, Miss Cassidy."

She smiles her wide, frank smile. "I hope so, Edith. You're a clever girl, an ambitious girl. We have such hopes for you."

I try not to look too obviously at the clock on the wood-paneled wall. I'll have to *run*.

By the time I let myself in with my latchkey, I'm out of breath. The hallway is dark, cool, and quiet around me. Mrs. Kearney has been and gone; I can tell because the tiles on the hall floor shine with damp mop swirls.

"Gil!" I call, setting my key on the hallstand. "Are you there?"

Silly question. He hasn't been outside yet. Some days he hasn't even been downstairs. I listen at the bottom of the stairs, but there is no sign of life.

I go into the parlor, but it's empty, the carpet recently swept, the fire laid for later. The room is chilly. Dining room, kitchen—I even check the scullery—all empty.

Upstairs, the bathroom door is ajar, but all the others are shut. The tiredness that's been stalking me all day suddenly catches up with me, and I wish I could go up the stairs to my own little attic bedroom, climb onto the bed with my book, and curl up for the afternoon, forgetting about everything else. But it's history after lunch, and I can't bear to get behind. Father keeps saying I should move into Mother's old room, to be nearer him and Gilbert, but I love my attic.

I knock on the door of Gil's room. "Gil?"

No answer. Perhaps he is asleep. I push the door open very softly.

The bed is empty, the counterpane smooth. The room is immaculate, only the bottles of pills and liniment on the bedside table showing that Gilbert is home. Only the curtains are a little disordered. I cross to the window to straighten them, and there, below me in the back garden, is a strange old man.

Gilbert. He hasn't seen me. He shuffles around the lawn, head bowed, shoulders stooped. He is dressed in flannels and one of Hugh's old jerseys. I move away from the window.

I go downstairs and let myself out the back door. Gilbert is still circling the lawn, but he starts when I step onto it.

"Edie! What are you—?" He slips on a pile of wet mulched leaves and reaches for the trunk of the apple tree to right himself. I spring forward to take his arm.

"I just wanted to make sure you were all right."

He frowns.

"I mean—it's a long day for you." Neither of us mentions

that the last time I spoke to him, it was three in the morning and he was screaming the house down. "What are you doing?"

He sighs. "Hiding from Mrs. Kearney. She keeps trying to tell me about Mr. Kearney's bowels."

"She's gone. It's safe."

He looses my arm, and we walk back toward the house. "Won't you get in a row for playing truant?" he asks.

"Upper fifths are allowed out at lunchtime." He always thinks I'm about *twelve*. Except at three in the morning.

"Well, you're going to be late getting back."

If I don't tell him about Piers now, Father will come in from the bank with today's newspaper, and Father always reads all the Irish regiments in the casualty lists, often aloud.

"Gil—there's something I have to tell you."

We both pause at the back door. I take a deep breath and decide just to tell it straight. "We were told at prayers this morning—Piers McBride has been killed."

Gilbert bends down to take off his muddy shoes. His fingers fumble with the laces. He reaches for the carpet slippers he has left waiting and slides his feet into them. He leans back on his haunches, ready to stand up, but looks as if he isn't quite able to. I want to offer him an arm, but I don't know if this is the right thing to do. In the end he uses the wall as support and uncurls his back slowly, with tightened lips.

"That's five," he says.

"Five?"

"From the team. Out of fifteen." He says it very casually. "A nice round third. I think that's slightly higher than average."

"Gil, please don't —"

"What?"

"I'm sorry — I didn't want you to find out from someone else. Shall I make some lunch?"

I already know I am not going back to school this afternoon. Father will write a note. Panic surges inside me at the thought of missing *more* work — history and French — but it's only one afternoon.

I make omelets. Neither of us eats with much enthusiasm, but it's something to do. It feels odd, eating alone with Gilbert. When we were children, we used to have nursery supper, but there were always three of us, and Hugh and Gilbert used to talk their unintelligible boy-talk and I would imagine stories in my head.

Gilbert pours the tea, and I try not to notice the tremor in his hand. He notices me not noticing, and I become very interested in the pattern on my teacup.

"Killed how?" he asks, setting the teapot down on its stand. A little tea slops out of the spout onto the tablecloth.

It takes me a moment to realize he means Piers. I frown, trying to remember Dr. Allen's exact words. "*Killed in action,* the doc said."

"Good."

I know what he means. *Killed in action* means it was likely to have been quick. And there will be a grave. Hugh was *Died of wounds:* the letter from the padre at the field hospital said he was operated on to amputate both legs, but died of a hemorrhage.

"Piers always wanted to join in with the big boys," Gilbert says. "Maybe he shouldn't have been let onto the first team so young, but he was so jolly talented we'd never have won the Schools Cup without him. He was a wonder." His voice is quite steady, but he frowns at the teapot. "You're *sure* it wasn't *Missing?*"

"Positive." When our cousin Edward was *Missing in action* at Loos, I was so young and stupid that I thought it just meant *lost.* I imagined him wandering about, or hiding, turning up when the battle was over. Hugh, on leave after his first spell at the front, had given a harsh laugh. "*Missing* means they can't find enough bits to put together to identify you."

I shake that memory off — I'd had nightmares for weeks — and fetch my satchel. I take the letter out of my *Othello* and hand it to Gilbert. He scans the single scrawled sheet and gives a fleeting grin. "Poor bugger." He bites his lip. "Sorry, Sis. Unsoldierly language — well, very soldierly language, actually."

"I've heard worse," I lie. "I'm not a kid."

"No. I don't suppose it's been much fun for you either, stuck here with Father."

"Not much."

"Are you going to give the letter to his family?"

"Yes. Patricia's in the sixth form." I have an inspiration.

"Would *you* take it?" I ask before I think better of it. "It might mean more coming from a fellow soldier. You've been there; you know what it was like. And you were friends."

Gilbert frowns. "It's rather soon. It might be intrusive."

But he sets the envelope very carefully on the mantelpiece behind the clock and shuffles off with yesterday's *News Letter.* Shortly I hear his heavy, uncertain tread on the stairs.

By the time I have cleared away lunch, it's only two. How can I fill the afternoon? Mrs. Kearney has left dinner ready as usual; my job is to start cooking it, but Father won't be home until almost six. I could catch up on all the prep I've missed lately. I do get as far as setting my books out around me at the dining-room table, but the room is cold, and dim even with the gas lit, and my eyes smart and prick with tiredness.

I'll bake some buns.

Baking wakes and warms me, and fills the house with a lovely homey smell. I set the little buns out to cool in the scullery and tidy the kitchen, pleased with my industry. My books are still sitting on the dining-room table. The Wars of the Roses. Latin. *Othello.*

The doorbell makes me jump and almost drop my Latin book. Gilbert won't think of opening it, even if he hears it from upstairs. He can't get used to the fact that we have no proper servants now. Last time he was at home, Annie would have answered it, but Annie makes shells now and says she wouldn't go back into service, not for a pension. I check that my skirt isn't floury and go to answer it.

It's Frank. He looks very young and very well, brushing the rain from the shoulders of his coat. "Edith. Is that face powder? Surely not."

I swipe at my face. "It's flour," I explain. I pull the door wide. "Come in."

He steps into the hall and hands me his hat and overcoat, damp with rain.

"What are you doing here?" I ask. I know I sound rude. What I would like to say is, *Gilbert has been home for ten days; he has had nobody to talk to except Father and me, and I am a girl and Father is old, so where on earth have* you *been?*

"I've come to see Gilbert, of course. Is he in?"

"He's always in. I don't know if he's seeing visitors, though. I'll have to ask. Follow me."

Something in the way he pushes back his dark hair—exactly like Maud's—from his forehead tells me he is more nervous than his manner reveals. Does he think Gilbert will hand him a white feather or give him a lecture about not joining up? Or is he simply nervous about meeting this new Gilbert?

"You must have been very busy with your studies," I say.

"I—yes. Otherwise I'd have called, of course. But actually—well, Maud told me about poor old Piers. And I thought . . ."

Better go and see the friends who are still alive.

I show Frank into the parlor. He sniffs the air. "What a lovely smell."

I soften a little. "I've been baking."

"How clever. Maud isn't the slightest bit domestic."

Lucky Maud, I think, but all I say is, "I'll make tea."

As his room is at the back, perhaps Gilbert didn't hear the door, because when I knock and say, "Gil? Frank is here," his reply sounds genuinely surprised.

"Frank?"

I put my head around the side of the door. He is lying on top of his bed, with an old dressing gown over his clothes, but already pulling himself up. I hand him his slippers, but he shakes his head and limps over to the wardrobe and pulls out a pair of shoes. He pulls off the old jersey, exchanges it for a sports coat, and checks himself in the glass.

"It's only *Frank.* You don't need to make yourself beautiful," I say. We both know it has nothing to do with vanity.

"I'll bring tea," I say as Gilbert opens the parlor door. I make tea and pile buns on a plate. I use the good tea set.

"You've only set it for two," Frank says when I come in with the tray.

"I'm sure you two have lots to catch up on. And I've prep to do."

"Maud never does any prep," Frank says. "But she did say you were brainy and want to go to college. There are lots of women students at Queen's now. I think it's super."

Gilbert looks at me in surprise. "College, Edie? You haven't mentioned that lately."

My cheeks burn, and I busy myself with pouring tea. "I must go and do my Latin. There's more hot water in the jug."

It's a tricky translation. I use Hugh's old dictionary, and I'm so busy looking up *renuntiare* that when Gilbert comes into the dining room in his outdoor clothes, I blink at him in confusion.

He crosses to the fireplace and takes the letter from behind the clock.

"We thought we'd go now," he says. "Frank's coming, too." I hear Frank in the hall, getting his outdoor things.

"To the McBrides'?"

He nods.

"Gil—it's pouring. You haven't been outside since—"

"I was outside today."

"You know what I mean—you're not fit."

"I'm fine."

"They live miles away."

"We'll get the tram. Don't *fuss*, Edie."

I know he doesn't want to seem like an invalid in front of Frank. And I suppose if you've come home from the Western

Front, getting a tram across Belfast isn't such an expedition. I make him take a woolen muffler.

It's such a miserable day that I draw down the blinds in the parlor, even though it's still light.

Father, arriving home at 5:50 p.m. exactly, is flabbergasted. "He went out with Frank? In *that*? When he can't make it up the stairs sometimes without resting?" He shakes his head. "He'll miss his dinner if he isn't back soon. What has Mrs. Kearney left for us today?"

"Croquettes. And there are some wee buns I made."

"You made buns?" He sounds pleased.

I tell him about leaving school early. "Gilbert was in such a state last night. I wanted to be sure he was all right. The days must be so long for him."

It's the first time I've ever mentioned Gilbert's nights. After the first two, when he stood helplessly in the doorway, Father has not gotten up. I don't think he can possibly have slept through—his room, Hugh's old room, is next door—but he leaves it to me.

Father isn't at all cross about my unauthorized half-day. "It's not as if it matters at this stage," he says.

"What do you mean?"

"Well, you're sixteen. There's no law keeping you at school."

"No law, but . . ." The college gates in my head creak and half close.

"Edith, love, let's eat. You can keep Gilbert's warm, can't you?"

We sit opposite each other at the dining table, just as we did all the months between Mother dying and Gilbert's return. I keep listening for the front door. They should be home by now.

Father nods at the bun on his plate, which I have given him with some custard. "Light as a feather, Edith. You're a grand wee housekeeper. When you leave school, you'll be able to take over all the cooking."

"Father—you know I want to stay on and go to college." *Think of the gates,* I will myself. *Keep them open.* They shudder on their hinges.

"I know there was some notion about it. But that was before."

I set my spoon down. It rings against the table mat. "*Mother* wanted me to go."

"But what about—?"

There is a loud chime from the doorbell. I jump up in relief. Gilbert must have forgotten his latchkey.

Gilbert sways in the doorway, looking as if only willpower is holding him upright. Rain streams off his hat, and his coat is sodden.

"I think—it was a bit far," he says, shambling into the hall.

I take his arm and half drag him into the parlor, where I lit the fire before dinner. He is shivering violently, his lips bluish and his breath ragged. "Sorry, Sis," he manages to say. "You were—right."

"Don't try to talk."

Gilbert collapses onto the settee, and I start to pull his soaking coat off. His limbs are shaking so badly that I prick my finger on the little silver lapel badge that shows he has served and been honorably discharged. I lick the drop of blood from my fingertip. Father watches.

"Father! Fetch some brandy," I order. "And run a hot bath. Put some mustard into it."

He scuttles off obediently. I pull off my woolen cardigan and wrap it around Gilbert's shoulders.

Father appears with a glass of brandy and then disappears again. I hear the roar of the hot-water cistern. I tilt the glass to Gilbert's lips. They chatter against it, but he manages to choke down some of the brandy. Very soon a tiny spot of color warms his face, and the shaking subsides slightly, so that he is able to hold the glass himself and take further sips.

"It was too far," he says again. "And when we got there—"

"Didn't they want to see you?"

"They were happy to see *me*."

"Ah."

"They didn't *say* anything—they were very polite. But it was so obvious that they despised him. And when we left—he was a bit rattled. He didn't want to get the tram—it was rush hour and he knew people would be staring at him, not in uniform. So we walked."

"You walked from the Cregagh Road?"

"It isn't that far. We cut through the Ormeau Park."

"But—"

All the times I have defended Frank, all the times I have told the indignant Maud that it must take a particular kind of courage for him not to join up—

"Where's the bold Frank now? I notice he didn't see you safely home."

"Edie—I'm not a child." He gives a sudden convulsive shiver.

"Come on—that bath must be ready now."

He goes to stand, but his back and legs don't seem to want to move. I have to take his arms and give him a hoist. When we reach the bottom of the stairs, he has to hold the rail in one hand and creep up, bent almost double. By the time we reach the bathroom door, sweat stands on his forehead and his lips are white with pain and effort.

I'm worried that I'm going to have to help him into the bath and out again. Surely Father . . . ?

It seems not.

More than an hour later, Gilbert is in bed. I go downstairs and tidy up the brandy glass and the remains of our abandoned dinner. Father sits at the table. He takes off his spectacles and rubs the wrinkled skin around his eyes.

"You were wonderful, Edith: you knew just what to do."

"Common sense."

"No. You've a grand way with you. You're a great wee nurse."

"I haven't finished my prep." Every unfinished Latin exercise, every unread poem, forces the gates just a little more shut.

"Och, that's not important. I'll write you a note."

I look in on Gilbert on my way up to bed. He is sleeping quietly, but still curled up as if he can't straighten without pain. I look into Mother's room. Its heavy dark furniture crouches in the shadows. It smells faintly of violets. I hurry past up the attic stairs.

I light the gas in my room. It's comfy in bed; I sit up with a bed jacket on and think briefly about my Latin prep. But I'm too tired.

I jerk awake. It's the usual shout, only louder tonight. Eyes still half closed, limbs leaden, I drag myself out of bed. The staircase outside my room is pitch-black; I have to feel my way down.

Gil is scrunched at the top of his bed, shaking, the blankets in a tangled heap on the floor. The first thing I do is pull them up to cover him. As soon as I put my hand on him, I realize this is more than the usual nightly terror. He is burning and shivering at the same time, his lips moving in a ceaseless mutter.

"Gil." I smooth back his drenched hair from his burning forehead. "It's all right. You're just dreaming."

His eyes stare beyond me, unfocused. "They're coming," he says hoarsely. "It can't be much longer now. They must be on their way." He sounds as if he is trying to reassure someone else.

"They're here *now*," I say. "It's all right." I pull him toward me, and his head rests briefly against my chest before he jerks it up again and shouts, "Don't go to sleep! You'll drown."

"I won't let anyone drown," I promise.

Father appears in the doorway in his old camel-hair dressing gown.

"Father," I say quietly, "we need the doctor."

"It's just a chill," Father says. "It was bound to happen, after that soaking."

"It's not just a chill. He's in agony."

Gilbert's body is twisted into something like, I suppose, the shape it must have been in his long vigil in the shell hole.

"Telephone *now*," I say. Father leaves.

I go to the bathroom and fetch a flannel and a basin of cool water, and start to sponge Gilbert's burning face. His pajamas are drenched in sweat, and however shy I feel, I know I must take them off and change them. The muttering has stopped; his harsh breathing is the only sound in the room apart from the occasional *putt-putt* of the gas lamp. I fetch clean pajamas, then begin the long, painful process of trying to bend Gilbert's spasming limbs without hurting him too much. Pretty soon, I'm the one sweating with the effort, and he is groaning with pain, his jaw set. He can't straighten his back, and even when he is in clean pajamas, he lies hunched like a question mark.

"The doctor's on his way," Father says. He stands in the doorway, looking helpless. "What can I do?"

"You could make some hot-water bottles," I say, thinking that heat around his limbs might help the pain and stiffness.

Dr. Bolton, small and fussy, has known us all our lives. He frowns at the state Gilbert's in, nods at what I have done to try to make him more comfortable, gives Gilbert some powders, and leaves some for me.

"Nasty thing, rheumatism like this," he says. "We don't usually see it in such young men, but . . ." He shakes his head and writes down instructions for me.

"Should we have a nurse?" I ask, crossing my fingers in hope behind my back.

"A *nurse*? Good gracious me, no. He'll be fine in a day or so. And I can see what a grand little nurse you are. Sixteen now, aren't you? Well, then. No point in messing up all your routines with a nurse. And I'm sure he would rather be looked after by his sister than a stranger. Eh, Gilbert, old chap?"

Whatever was in the powder Dr. Bolton made up must be starting to take effect, because Gilbert gives a tired grin and says, "The nurses in France were dragons."

I have a sudden memory of Maud—was it only this morning?—impatient to do something in the war, wanting to nurse soldiers. I won't see her tomorrow. I have to stay at home and look after Gilbert.

And the next day, and the next.

He will get better. He will get better than he is tonight. But he will never be the boy who left here in 1915, and he will never be the person he would have been without the war.

And neither will I.

Father goes down to show Dr. Bolton out. I go to the window and look into the garden, sepia in the cold March dawn. I stifle a yawn. It would make sense to see out what's left of the night in Mother's old room. I go in and close the door tight behind me, breathing in the scent of dust and violets. Father's right: it's silly to be up in the attic when it's so far from the rest of the family.

Previous page: **FIGHTER PLANES**

In 1917, Germany began bombing raids against Britain using aircraft rather than zeppelins. Aircraft raids were deadlier than zeppelin raids, so Britain's defense strategy had to evolve. Fighter planes were sent to combat enemy aircraft, and anti-aircraft guns became more sophisticated.

LITTLE

> You have only to play at Little Wars three or four times to realize just what a blundering thing Great War must be.
> — H. G. Wells, Little Wars (1913)

All that summer, Jemima's brother, March, spent every day playing with toy soldiers in the backyard. He dug up a big pile of dirt and shaped it into mountains and cliffs and narrow dark caves. He snapped short branches from the lemon tree and stuck them into brown crumbling hillsides. He made

WARS

URSULA DUBOSARSKY

craters in the earth with his hands and filled them with water from the garden tap so they formed little puddly lakes. He built houses from pieces of sandstone and stray fence palings.

"What are you doing?" asked Jemima, standing on a patch of bare grass, watching him.

"It's a battlefield," said March shortly, not even glancing up.

He began positioning the soldiers, one by one—on the mountains, next to the lakes, hidden inside the houses and caves. The soldiers were made of metal, painted in red and blue and green, in helmets and coats and black boots. They stood or knelt with guns; they marched with rifles over their shoulders; they held flags; they saluted; they lay flat on their bellies, ready to crawl and shoot. Some were on horseback; others pushed cannons. One held both hands up in surrender, and another was thrust backward, flinching at the moment of death.

"Jemima!" called her mother. "Leave March alone and come inside!"

Jemima turned around on one leg, hopping on the spot.

"Jemima!" called her mother again.

Jemima sighed. She headed for the house, still hopping, but backward so she could keep looking. When she got inside, she stood up on a kitchen chair and pressed her nose against the glass, staring out. She couldn't take her eyes off the toy soldiers.

Their father had brought the toy soldiers home one day on the tram from work. He came in the front door just before dinner and took off his black hat and pulled out a brown paper parcel from under his coat. Inside was a long wooden box with a sliding lid, the sort of box you might keep pencils in.

"March," he said, "I've got something for you. Come and have a look."

March and Jemima ran over. Their father sat down on a stool and slid the lid of the box open. The little soldiers lay there, one on top of the other, their pale, brave faces staring upward.

"I got them from a fellow on the street in town," their father said.

"From a fellow?" said Jemima's mother.

Their mother was tall and wore beautiful long skirts and blouses so white it was as though she must have washed them in milk.

"Ay, you know, some poor fellow," their father replied, grimacing.

There were lots of poor fellows on the street in town. Jemima had seen them: standing, sitting on boxes or blankets, asking for money in exchange for little bunches of flowers or cards. Poor fellows without arms and legs, even without eyes. Poor fellows, back from the war.

"They've given their everything," Miss Martingale said at school, her hand on her heart, staring stonily through black-rimmed glasses at the Union Jack and the portrait of the king above it. "Look at what they have given, children. They have given their everything. And some will never come back. You must always remember Gallipoli, children," Miss Martingale said, and the word rang like a magic spell in Jemima's head — *Gallip-oh-lee Gallip-oh-lie Gallip-oh-lee Gallip-oh-lie Gallip-oh-lee Gallip-oh-lie Gallip-oh-lee Gallip-oh-lie* . . .

But those poor fellows on the street were real soldiers. The soldiers in the box were toys. Her mother saw Jemima's expression as March held out his hands to his father.

"You have your own games, Jemmy," she said gently. "These are for March."

Jemima nodded. Of course, she knew the soldiers would be for March. But nodding couldn't stop her from wanting them.

Word soon spread about March's soldiers. It was the holidays, and boys from the surrounding houses turned up to see. They wandered through the side gate, down the path to the backyard.

March was very proud. He walked around the battlefield, pointing things out and making long explanations. He knew a lot about armies and battles. The boys put the soldiers in different positions and built and rebuilt the falling mountainsides. Jemima hid behind the lemon tree, watching and listening, smelling the lemony scent of the blossoms.

After a few days, the boys lost interest and wandered off

again. All except one, a boy named Arly. He lived three doors down from them, alone with his mother in a house surrounded by overgrown banana trees thick as a jungle, full of possums and ibis nests. Arly had very short hair and mean eyes. Jemima was afraid of him. One morning he came down the side path to the backyard carrying a burlap bag. March was crouching on the ground next to the battlefield.

"Morning, Arly," said March, looking up and nodding.

Arly said nothing, but stopped next to the largest mountain and opened the bag. Out tumbled an army of toy soldiers in a pile onto the soft earth.

"We can make a war," said Arly. "Yours against mine."

He looked at March, challenging him. Excited, March sprang up at once and began looking through Arly's soldiers. They were a mixed bunch. Some were painted and peeling; some had no color at all. Some had arms broken off or were missing their rifles.

"Where did you get them?"

"They're my dad's," said Arly.

March was silent. From her hiding position behind the lemon tree, Jemima knew why. It was because Arly's father had gone to the war. He had gone with all the other soldiers, marching past the big post office, their feet stamping in heavy boots. They marched all the way down to the edge of the ocean, to get on a boat to go to the war.

Jemima's mother had taken her and March into town that day to see the soldiers go. It was raining, and there were so many umbrellas and there was music from a brass band and shouting and laughing and crying as well as the endless stamping of feet. Not all the soldiers marched—there were slow-moving trams crammed full of them, and they leaned out the windows and hung off the doors in their funny half-folded hats.

Jemima's mother had given her a little Union Jack to wave. As she stood there with her flag on the side of the road, suddenly, from one of the trams, huge strong arms reached down and pulled her right off the ground. For a moment the world turned upside down, like the swing in the playground at school when it sailed too high in the air over the jacaranda tree.

It was Arly's father! Jemima stared in amazement as he held her up in his arms. Arly's father was a soldier! Why, last time she had seen him, he was in a jacket and tie, going to work like all the other fathers. How could he suddenly turn into a soldier? It was as though he were in a costume.

"Can you believe it—little Jem!" said Arly's father, and he turned to the other soldiers. They smelled of sweat and beer. "My neighbor's kid!"

There were tears in his green eyes, shiny like wet fish. He hugged her tight, and she felt his big heart pounding under the scratchy wool of his uniform. Then he kissed her in the middle of her cheek and let her down on the street again. The slow-moving tram bore him away, laughing and waving, while the brass band followed down the long road and around the corner to the great wide Pacific Ocean, away, away.

"Well, goodness, what an extraordinary thing to do!" said her mother, pulling Jemima close to her skirts. "Arly's father. And in all this crowd, he spotted you!"

Jemima was trembling.

"Dad won't be a soldier, will he?" she said, grabbing her mother's hand. "Will he?"

Jemima's mother wore a huge hat covered with flowers that hid her long, dark hair pinned up to her neck. She didn't answer, but there was a sort of smile on her lips, and Jemima was sure that the smile said, *No, of course not, don't be silly; your father can't be a soldier. He has to stay with us, in our world.*

That was a long time ago — why, it was almost a year. *Gallip-oh-lee Gallip-oh-lie Gallip-oh-lee Gallip-oh-lie.* Now the two boys, Arly and March, huddled together discussing in low, serious voices their plans for battle.

"With two armies," said March, "we can make them fight each other."

"That's right," said Arly. "We can make a real war."

He bent down and picked up one of the soldiers.

"This is the best one," he said. "I call him the General. He's not really a general — that's just what I call him."

He held the soldier up carefully, turning it around.

"It's worth a bit of money, I reckon," said Arly. "My dad sent it over. You know."

Again, March was respectfully silent for a moment as he inspected it. "Pretty fine," he agreed, and whistled.

Jemima couldn't help it. She had to see the General. She began to creep forward on all fours, out from behind the lemon tree, across the ragged earth, over to where the boys were. Summer light shone on the General's bright-blue coat and his tall black boots. His back was straight and strong, and he held a rifle over his shoulder. Jemima crept even closer. If she could just see his face —

"Jemima!"

Too late! Her mother was rapping firmly on the kitchen window. Reluctantly, Jemima got up on her feet. She sighed. She would have to go inside again.

March and Arly hardly gave her a glance. They turned to the battlefield. Their minds were full.

After that, Arly came every day. The sun rose high and hot, and by eight o'clock Arly was there. He didn't knock but went straight down the side of the house to the backyard and waited for March.

"Morning, March," Arly would say in his mean voice as March came out, wiping his just-washed face.

"Morning, Arly," March would reply.

Together they surveyed the battleground, kicking away loose stones, righting the trees that the neighborhood cats or possums had pushed over in the night. Then, when everything was ready, the two of them would lie on their stomachs in the grass and dirt, attacking each other's armies with little seesaw catapults made out of spoons and pebbles, making the sounds of warfare: gunshots and cannonballs, shouts of triumph and death cries.

Jemima sat as near to the battlefield as she could, out of sight of her mother, her knees drawn up to her chest, pulling her hat right over her head against scorching beams of the summer sun. The boys knew she was there. Occasionally March would get her to fetch a can of water to fill up a dried lake or replace the shriveled branches with fresh green cuttings from the lemon tree.

When this happened, she could see the soldiers closer up. It was funny how they all had different faces, different ways of looking. Some stared out very bravely, some looked nervous, some looked as though they were angry, and others about to laugh. Some gazed ahead into the distance almost as though they were blind and not seeing anything at all.

One day a blow from the catapult was so strong that it knocked the head of one of the soldiers right off. Jemima felt sick and almost screamed, but March and Arly took it more calmly. They frowned and then started looking for the pieces.

"We can melt the metal on the fire in the kitchen," said Arly when he had found the head of the unlucky soldier at the bottom of one of the little lakes. "Then stick the two bits back together again."

March nodded approvingly, and the boys went inside with the pieces. While they were gone, Jemima crept forward slowly on her knees until she reached the battlefield. Then she crouched down as low as she could, right next to the General. He had a black mustache and a sharp little nose. He looked neither brave nor frightened, but somehow sad, just sad.

She reached forward and picked him up, just for a moment while no one was looking, and held him tight in her fingers. He felt heavy and cold, like money.

The next day, as Jemima was about to head out to the backyard, her mother tugged her braid and said, "You've got a friend coming this morning."

A friend?

"Who?" Jemima asked suspiciously.

"Mary Dean," said her mother. "Her big sister's bringing her over. She'll be here soon."

Mary Dean? Jemima groaned.

"Why?" she said, annoyed, kicking the skirting board.

"You need to have your own friends, Jemima," her mother said firmly. "You can't spend your life watching the boys play."

Mary Dean's not my friend, Jemima wanted to say, although that was not quite true. Mary Dean was sort of a friend. She had red hair and strange yellow teeth. They sat together at school; they played hopscotch together in the playground. But what would she do all morning with Mary Dean?

She need not have worried. Mary Dean came fully prepared. When they opened the door to let her in, she drew from her pinafore pocket a long pair of sharp scissors.

"Do you have any newspaper?" Mary Dean asked, waving the scissors around.

Jemima's mother quickly found her some old newspapers. Mary Dean sat down on the floor in the front room cutting up the sheets of newspaper into long strips. Some were as long as a person. She never got sick of cutting. She was very determined.

After a while Jemima sighed and said, "Do you want to go outside and see the chickens?"

"All right," said Mary Dean, putting down the scissors. "For a while, anyway."

The two girls pulled on their sun hats and went out the back door into the yard. Mary Dean frowned at March and Arly, who were jumping around, shouting and throwing missiles at each other's soldiers. She put her hands over her ears.

Jemima led her to the henhouse, which was at the end of

the garden. She tugged open the wire door and stepped inside, Mary Dean following gingerly behind her. The three red hens, Lucky, Clucky, and Bendigo, ran forward, bobbing their heads up and down.

"I don't like hens," said Mary Dean, quickly jumping backward.

Jemima sank down into the hay, and Clucky settled comfortably in her lap. She peered through the chicken wire at the two boys in the distance as they repositioned their armies around the battlefield.

"I might go back inside now," said Mary Dean, "and finish my cutting."

"All right," said Jemima, stroking Clucky's soft feathers. "I'll stay here for a while."

After lunch, Mary Dean's big sister came and took her and her big pair of scissors home. Jemima helped her mother pick up all the pieces of newspaper from the floor of the front room and put them in a box for scrap. It took a long time, as there were so many pieces, and some were very thin.

"That is an odd child," said Jemima's mother.

Jemima understood with relief that this meant her mother would not invite Mary Dean over again. After all, by herself she didn't make any mess at all. She was fully occupied just watching the boys and the toy soldiers.

One night, Jemima was woken by a great downpour of summer rain drumming on the roof. The window above her bed was half open, and water was splashing onto her blanket. She sat up and pushed the window closed. March, who slept in the bed next to her, lay undisturbed, flat on his back with his arms above his head.

Jemima thought of all the soldiers outside on the battlefield, poor cold things. She imagined the General's shiny blue coat getting wetter and wetter. She fell asleep again.

In the morning, it was still raining but more lightly. Jemima put on her pinafore and boots and went to the laundry to find her father's big black umbrella. She slipped out the laundry door to the backyard. She wanted to get there before Arly and March, to see how the soldiers had survived the night. She came to a halt in shock at the sight before her. She threw the open umbrella on the ground and walked slowly over.

The battlefield was destroyed. The mountains had crumbled and collapsed into mud; the trees were blown away; the lakes were overflowing. The little soldiers had fallen this way and that and were upside down, half buried, or had completely disappeared under the deluge.

Jemima knelt down in the mud. She pulled out one of the drowning soldiers from where he lay, up through the rubble and dirt. He looked terrible. She rubbed the mud off him with the edge of her pinafore and then stood him up again.

She found another. She pulled him up by his little arm, which was tightly hanging on to his rifle. She cleaned him up, too, and stood him next to the first. Then she found another and did the same again. And then another.

There were so many, she decided to gather them in the pocket of her pinafore. She sat down on the wet ground and took them out one at a time, dipping them in the water of the lake, wiping away the mud, and drying them off. Then she separated them into the two armies, March's and Arly's. Soon they formed two long lines, shiny and ready for battle.

"What are you doing?"

Jemima jolted. She swung around. It was Arly.

"You've moved them!"

He strode over to her, his eyes spitting. She stumbled to her feet.

"I was just saving them," she said. She could hear her own voice trembling. He looked so angry. "The rain made everything fall down."

What was wrong? She hadn't hurt them.

"You've moved them," repeated Arly in his meanest voice.

The black umbrella tumbled about in the morning wind. The rain had completely stopped now, apart from a few stray drops. Arly's whole body was stiff with fury. For a moment, Jemima thought he was going to hit her.

"What's up?"

The back screen door swung open. It was March, awake and dressed.

Instinctively Jemima leaped toward him. She opened her mouth, but no words came out.

"Look what she's done," snarled Arly, gesturing. "She's ruined the game."

March came over to the desolate landscape, his hands in his pockets. He did not pay attention to Jemima. He stared somberly at the demolished mountains, the fallen houses and trees, and the overflowing lakes. Then he turned and looked at the two lines of rescued soldiers.

"She's moved all the men," said Arly. He sounded so cold. "If she'd left them where they were, we could have worked it out. Now the game is completely ruined."

Jemima didn't understand. How was it ruined? "Worked what out?"

March sighed. But she could tell he was angry, too.

"We're not just playing with toys, like you do," he said. "This is a real war. It's very important where each soldier is. We keep score. Each soldier gets different points. This battle's been going on for days. Now we'll have to start all over again."

Jemima felt sick, and her face grew red with shame.

"I didn't know—" she began, but March turned his back on her.

"Just go away, will you?" he snapped. "Go away."

Jemima stomped away, but not inside. She didn't want to face her mother and the questions she would ask. Instead she went to the henhouse and hid herself in the corner, under the damp straw. Lucky, Clucky, and Bendigo stepped curiously over to her, but she turned her face to the wall.

She had just wanted to help. Now they hated her; both boys hated her. They didn't have to be so mean. She hated them back. She pulled up the edge of her filthy pinafore to wipe the tears from her eyes.

That was when she realized that she still had one of the rescued soldiers in her pinafore pocket. She pulled him out. It was the General. He lay in her hand on his back, staring sadly up at the sky.

March and Arly spent the rest of the morning rebuilding the battlefield. After the rain, the day turned terribly hot, and the sun burned their faces as they dug the dirt with spades, and molded the mountains and cliff faces, and reconstructed the walls of the lake with sticks and pebbles.

Jemima crept out of the henhouse, back to her spot behind the lemon tree to watch. She couldn't help herself.

Once the battlefield was restored, it was a matter of positioning the troops. The two boys painstakingly began to put the soldiers in their places on the mountains and in the crevices. The water of the lake lapped around them, like a huge sea.

March was counting the soldiers. The numbers had to be even, so it would be a fair fight.

"One's missing," he said.

He took off his hat and wiped the sweat from his freckled face. Arly was counting the soldiers too, squatting on the ground. He touched each soldier with his finger as he counted. When he stood up, his eyes had an odd expression.

"It's the General," he said. "The General's missing."

March looked at the huge mountain they had rebuilt.

"Oh, Lord," he said. "Don't tell me he's buried under all that!"

The two boys gazed at each other.

"I don't reckon he's under there," said Arly.

March frowned, questioningly.

"I reckon she took it," said Arly.

He knew Jemima was behind the lemon tree.

"What?" said March. "Jemima?"

"Your sister," said Arly. "I reckon she took it."

"She wouldn't do that," said March.

"She took it," said Arly doggedly.

He turned and began to walk toward Jemima's hiding place. She felt a terrible fear all through her body, but she couldn't move. Arly darted forward suddenly and grabbed her shoulder.

"You took the General," he hissed. "I know you did."

Jemima shook her head.

"Show me your pocket!"

Silently, Jemima displayed her pinafore pocket. There was nothing in it but a few twigs and pieces of straw.

"Leave her alone," said March, coming over. "She wouldn't take it. Leave her alone."

Arly let go of Jemima. He turned and faced March, his fingers rolled into a fist. He punched March in the middle of his face.

Jemima screamed. Her mother came running out from the kitchen, where she was putting out the jam for scones. She still had the spoon in her hand with the jam sticking to it.

"For heaven's sake," she cried. "Stop that! I won't have it."

Arly let his fist fall. He cast his eyes down to the ground. He went over to where his burlap bag lay folded near the back door of the house, and then picked up each of his soldiers from the battlefield and packed them in the bag, one by one.

Nobody spoke. When all the soldiers were back in the bag, Arly walked quickly down the side passage and was gone. They heard the gate clanging shut.

"What on earth was that all about?" asked Jemima's mother. "What upset him so?"

Neither of them answered. March went inside, banging the door. Jemima stood, clinging onto the trunk of the tree, almost as though she had become part of the tree itself.

In the morning when Jemima went down for breakfast, she saw her mother and father with March at the kitchen table. The newspaper was spread open across it.

"Poor woman," said her mother, shaking her head. "Poor boy. No wonder yesterday —"

She saw Jemima and broke off.

"What is it?"

Nobody spoke. Jemima leaned over her father's shoulder and looked at the newspaper. There were all the faces, the soldiers in their half-folded hats, staring out at the world. *Dead dead dead,* said Miss Martingale. *They have given their everything,* said Miss Martingale. *Gallip-oh-lee Gallip-oh-lie Gallip-oh-lee Gallip-oh-lie Gallip-oh-lee Gallip-oh-lie . . .*

"Arly's father is missing," said Jemima's father, tapping the kitchen table.

Her mother went to the window and put the palms of her hands on the glass. Jemima suddenly felt very heavy, from her head to her feet.

"It means he's dead," said March. His voice cracked. "Doesn't it, Dad?"

"It means they can't find him," said their father.

"I'll take March down to see them," said Jemima's mother, from the window. Her voice sounded far away.

"It's the least we can do."

It was so strange, thought Jemima, to know that someone you knew had died when the room was filled with the smell of toast and frying eggs, the sounds of a chair scraping and the page of the newspaper turning. You would think the world would be as still and silent as a church in the middle of the night, but it wasn't. The world wasn't like that.

When her mother returned with March, they were both very quiet. March lay down on the couch in the front room and closed his eyes.

"They're leaving," said Jemima's mother. "They're going to live with her sister. Ah, dear."

She took off her hat, slowly and carefully.

"They're leaving their house?" asked Jemima's father. "They're moving away?"

"Yes," said her mother. She smoothed out the flowers of her hat, petal by petal.

"They were packing while we were there. They'll be gone within an hour. They knew yesterday, you see, before it was in the paper. The postman brought a letter."

Everyone knew about those letters, those dreadful letters, lined in black.

"Arly knew yesterday?" said Jemima, disbelieving.

She couldn't understand it. Arly knew that his father was

dead? Why didn't he tell them? Why did he come to play and act as if nothing had happened?

"Shhh, Jemmy," said her mother. "Let's have some quiet."

She sank down in an armchair and closed her eyes, like March.

Jemima left the room, straight out the back door, past the battlefield, all the way to the henhouse. She stepped over Lucky, Clucky, and Bendigo, almost tripping in her hurry. She knelt down next to their nesting box and plunged her hand in, feeling blindly around the straw. There was a clutch of fresh eggs, but that was not what she was looking for.

At last, from the depths of the warm nest, she pulled out the General.

By the time Jemima reached the house surrounded by the banana trees, thick with tightly bunched green fruit, she could see that Arly and his mother were ready to leave. Their belongings were piled high on a cart, and Arly's mother, dressed all in black, her shoulders hunched, was sitting at the front with the driver. Jemima couldn't see her face, as it was covered with a dark shawl.

Arly came out of the house, a satchel slung over his shoulder. He was wearing a black suit. He looked so old. Jemima felt something stabbing inside her, in her heart.

"Hello," she said.

Arly's face was blank. For a moment, Jemima thought he

was going to walk right past her, but he didn't. He stopped on the path next to the low little gate.

"We're going away," he said.

Jemima nodded.

"To live with my auntie."

Jemima nodded again.

"My dad's missing. That means he's dead."

Jemima opened her mouth. The air of the world moved through her and turned into breath. Breath turned into words.

"He might not be dead," she burst out. "He could just be lost."

Arly did not answer.

"Someone might have found him," said Jemima. "And they're hiding him. They're looking after him, until it's safe."

Arly straightened his shoulders. He went through the little gate and closed it carefully. Then he tossed his satchel on top of all their other things on the wagon, and pulled himself up after it.

"Good-bye," he said.

He was so high above her, and the sun dazzled her eyes. Now she had to do it. She reached into her pinafore pocket and pulled out the General.

"I'm sorry," she said.

She held up the little soldier to him flat on the palm of her hand. Arly stared down at it silently. Then he said, "I knew you took him."

Previous page: **MINES AND U-BOAT**
Moored underwater mines were used throughout the war to defend coasts, ports, and naval bases around the world. The mines exploded when they came into contact with a ship or submarine. Germany laid mines along shipping routes to sink ships carrying supplies to Britain. And to stop German U-boats, British and American ships laid 72,000 mines between Scotland and Norway; after the war, it took eighty-two ships five months to clear them.

This page: **ABANDONED HORSE**

Horses were indispensable to both sides during the war. They were ridden into battle, they carried supplies, and they pulled guns and ambulances. New Zealand gunner Bert Stokes said he was told in 1917 that "to lose a horse was worse than losing a man, because men were replaceable, while horses weren't, at that stage." However, when the war ended, horses were no longer needed. Many were abandoned or sold for meat.

Jemima couldn't answer. She was too ashamed. The driver of the cart cracked his whip. Arly's mother began to sob.

"Keep it," said Arly, and his eyes were green and shiny like wet fish. "It's just a toy. I don't want it anymore."

The driver cracked his whip again, and the brown horse began to trot off down the street, the cart trundling behind it. Jemima's fingers closed around the General, and her arm dropped to her side. She heard the clopping of the hooves and the turning of the wheels and the magpies swooping and crying above her head.

"You're wrong!" she shouted, running after the cart. "You're wrong!"

But it was no good. The cart was too fast. Arly was carried with it, away into the distance, beyond the sound of her voice. Soon there was nothing remaining but a huge cloud of dust.

"You're wrong," she said again, standing alone in the middle of the stony road. "You're wrong. He's not dead."

Arly's father was alive. Jemima knew it, quite suddenly. She knew it the same way she knew she was alive herself.

Because as she stood there, with her fingers closed tight around the body of the little General, she could feel, beneath his uniform, the unmistakable beating of a tiny heart.

ABOUT THE ITEMS

The objects that inspired the stories in this collection are tangible reminders of the war and the individuals behind the statistics. Some, such as the compass and the writing case, can still be used. From their appearance, it is hard to believe that they were made during a war that began a hundred years ago.

Brodie Helmet

"Our Jacko"

Michael Morpurgo

In the first year of the war, troops were not provided with steel hats, resulting in a huge number of lethal head wounds. The French army introduced steel helmets in 1915, and Englishman

John Leopold Brodie designed the Brodie helmet in the same year. The helmet was officially known as *Helmet, steel, Mark I* in Britain and the M1917 helmet in the United States. Colloquially, it was called the Tommy helmet, tin hat, or doughboy helmet. The German army called it the *Salatschüssel* (salad bowl). The helmet pictured above was worn by a soldier from the 1st Battalion, Lancashire Fusiliers, on the first day of the Battle of the Somme, when the battalion lost 486 men.

Compass

"Another Kind of Missing"

A. L. Kennedy

By the end of the war, weapons and military equipment were the most sophisticated they had ever been, but at first the sheer number of soldiers joining up meant there were serious shortages of weapons, uniforms, and equipment. Sometimes there weren't enough guns for soldiers to train with, so they often used dummy rifles made of wood. Soldiers had to provide some pieces of equipment themselves—for instance, all officers were expected to carry a compass. Pictured here is a 1916 Verners Pattern VII compass, which once belonged to Lieutenant C. Birdwood of the 3rd Battalion, Devon Regiment.

Nose of a Zeppelin Bomb

"Don't Call It Glory"

Marcus Sedgwick

In 1914, planes had existed for only ten years and air bombing raids seemed more like science fiction than reality. In 1915, Germany launched a fleet of zeppelin airships to drop fire bombs on London. They hovered only a few hundred meters over the city, but it seemed impossible to shoot them down; planes didn't move quickly enough, and bullets caused hardly any damage. In 1917, after two years of zeppelin raids, new bullets were invented that ignited the gas inside the zeppelins, destroying them, and the threat from zeppelins was effectively over. Pictured above is the nose cap from a zeppelin bomb that fell on Streatham, England, on September 24, 1916, killing a donkey.

Recruitment Poster

"The Country You Called Home"

John Boyne

At the start of the war, propaganda was still fairly crude, but as the war progressed, posters and other propaganda became more sophisticated. Many recruitment drives encouraged men to sign up with their friends, promising that those who "joined together should serve together" in "pals battalions." Recruitment drives for these battalions often appealed to local and ethnic identities, as this 1914 poster shows. Four Tyneside Irish battalions of the Northumberland Fusiliers were raised by this recruitment drive.

Princess Mary's Gift Fund Box

"When They Were Needed Most"

Tracy Chevalier

In 1914, seventeen-year-old Princess Mary set up a fund to provide those serving at the front or in the navy with Christmas gifts. Over £162,500 was raised to make Princess Mary's Gift Fund boxes. Most tins were for smokers and contained cigarettes.

Nonsmokers received candy and a writing case. All the tins included a Christmas card and a photograph of Princess Mary. At Christmas there was an unofficial truce, and Germans and Allied troops met in no-man's-land to play soccer and exchange gifts, including items from the boxes.

Soldier's Writing Case

"A World That Has No War in It"

David Almond

By 1918, the Army Postal Service employed 4,000 soldiers who made daily deliveries of morale-boosting letters to those serving on the front lines. Most soldiers wrote home as well, though their letters were censored so that they did not give away official secrets, and the soldiers themselves often decided to conceal the realities of life in the trenches from their families. The writing case pictured below belonged to Lieutenant-Colonel Frederick Heneker. He died on the first day of the Battle of the Somme, July 1, 1916, while commanding the 21st Northumberland Fusiliers.

Sheet Music

"A Harlem Hellfighter and His Horn"

Tanya Lee Stone

When the United States declared war on Germany in 1917, many African Americans rushed to join up. Black men served in separate army regiments from their white counterparts and weren't allowed to join the Marines. One of the most famous African-American regiments was the 369th Infantry Regiment, known as the Harlem Hellfighters. The regiment's band was directed by James Reese Europe, an influential band leader who helped open up music as a career to African Americans. The band traveled across France, entertaining American, British, and French troops and starting a craze for ragtime music in Europe. When the regiment returned home to the United States, they were given a heroes' welcome. Picured here is the sheet music for two of the Harlem Hellfighters' most popular songs.

War-Time Butter Dish

"Maud's Story"

Adèle Geras

The First World War led to food shortages in all the nations involved. Food production fell, and naval blockades and submarine warfare affected food imports. In Russia, Turkey, and Austria, there was widespread starvation and malnutrition, but France, Italy, and Britain introduced successful rationing systems. This British butter dish bears a message from the prime minister, encouraging people to be economical with food. The back reads: "The War Time Butter Dish for a family of ten. Made by the girls of Staffordshire during the winter of 1917 when the boys were in the trenches fighting for liberty and civilization."

Victoria Cross

"Captain Rosalie"

Timothée de Fombelle

The Victoria Cross is the highest award for bravery for British and Commonwealth servicemen. Of 1,357 Crosses that have been awarded, 634 were given during World War I. Pictured here is the Victoria Cross awarded to Boy, 1st Class, John Travers Cornwell for his actions in the Battle of Jutland on May 31, 1916. His ship was badly damaged by German gunfire, and every member of his gun crew was killed or wounded. Cornwell was hit in the chest by a shell fragment but stayed at his post, awaiting orders, until the ship was disengaged from the action. He died two days after the battle, on June 2, 1916, at age sixteen.

School Magazines

"Each Slow Dusk"

Sheena Wilkinson

School magazines published during World War I depicted, among rugby and hockey reports and news of exam success, the involvement of former students and teachers in the war. They often included excerpts of letters from the front and the obituaries of those who had lost their lives in the fighting. Pictured below is a collection of magazines published by Methodist College Belfast, from 1914 to 1919. In 1914, the mood was enthusiastic and patriotic; by 1916, the magazines were dominated by news of the dead and injured; and in 1919 the war wasn't mentioned at all.

French Toy Soldier
"Little Wars"

Ursula Dubosarsky

In the years leading up to World War I, toy soldiers became more and more popular as they became cheaper to produce. The toys appealed to adults as well as children, and in Britain, H. G. Wells published a popular set of war-game rules under the title *Little Wars*. The popularity of these toys may partly explain the enthusiasm for war when it broke out in 1914, and the number of men who so willingly volunteered to fight. This 1917 model of a French infantryman, or *poilu*, was sold in Paris for 70 francs. The soldier is dressed in the "horizon-blue" uniform of the French army.

PICTURE CREDITS

Object photographs copyright © by the Imperial War Museums (EPH 2780, EPH 9430, EPH 6282, EPH 3788, PST 13620, EPH 1992, OMD 2406, UNI 12606) except compass, copyright © 2014 by Walker Books Ltd.; sheet music, courtesy of the Library of Congress; and school magazines, copyright © 2014 by Sheena Wilkinson.

Opposite page: **FORD MODEL T FIELD AMBULANCE**
The first motorized ambulances were used during World War I.
Thousands of men and women volunteered as ambulance drivers
with the Red Cross, the American Field Service, and other
organizations. Famous ambulance drivers include the animator
Walt Disney, writers Ernest Hemingway and Somerset Maugham,
and the composer Maurice Ravel.

ABOUT THE
CONTRIBUTORS

Photo by Sara Jane Palmer

DAVID ALMOND worked as a teacher before becoming a full-time writer. His books for children include *Skellig, My Name Is Mina, The Boy Who Swam with Piranhas,* and *Mouse Bird Snake Wolf.* He has won numerous awards for his work, including the Hans Christian Andersen Award, a Carnegie Medal, two Whitbread Children's Book Awards, and a Michael L. Printz Award. He lives in northern England with his family.

JOHN BOYNE is the author of eight novels for adults and four for young readers, including *The Boy in the Striped Pajamas* and *Stay Where You Are and Then Leave,* both works of wartime fiction. *The Boy in the Striped Pajamas* has sold more than five million copies worldwide and was made into an award-winning film. John Boyne's work is published in more than forty-five languages. He lives in Dublin, Ireland.

Photo by Rich Gilligan

TRACY CHEVALIER is the author of seven novels, most recently *The Last Runaway.* She is best known for the international bestseller *Girl with a Pearl Earring,* which has sold more than five million copies, been translated into thirty-nine languages, and been made into a film. She grew up in Washington, D.C., and in 1984 moved to London, where she lives with her husband and son. She is a Fellow of Britain's Royal Society of Literature.

URSULA DUBOSARSKY is the author of more than thirty books for children. She has won several Australian book prizes, including the NSW, Victorian, South Australian, and Queensland Premier's literary awards. Her latest novels for young adults are *The Red Shoe*, set during a 1954 Australian spy scandal, and *The Golden Day*, set in a girls' school in 1967. She lives in Sydney, Australia, with her family.

TIMOTHÉE DE FOMBELLE is a popular French playwright and has achieved international success as a fiction author with *Toby Alone*, *Toby and the Secrets of the Tree*, and *Vango: Between Sky and Earth*. He lives in Paris with his family.

ADÈLE GERAS was born in Jerusalem and lived in Cyprus, Nigeria, and North Borneo as a child. She has written more than ninety books for children and young adults, including *Happy Ever After*, *Ithaka*, *A Thousand Yards of Sea*, and *Troy*, which was short-listed for the Whitbread Children's Book Award and the Carnegie Medal. She has also written four novels for adults. She lives in Cambridge, England.

JIM KAY worked in the archives of Tate Britain and the Royal Botanic Gardens before becoming a full-time illustrator. He received a Kate Greenaway Medal for his illustrations of Patrick Ness's *A Monster Calls,* and he was chosen by J. K. Rowling to illustrate the full-color editions of the Harry Potter series. He lives in Northamptonshire, England.

A. L. KENNEDY is the author of six novels, three works of nonfiction, and five short-story collections, including *All the Rage.* Her novel *Day* was named a Costa Book of the Year, and she has twice been selected as one of *Granta*'s Best of Young British Novelists. She is a Fellow of Britain's Royal Society of Arts and Royal Society of Literature. She is also a dramatist and writes a blog with the *Guardian.* She lives in London.

Photo by Campbell Mitchell

MICHAEL MORPURGO has written more than a hundred books, including *Meeting Cezanne, The Mozart Question,* and *I Believe in Unicorns.* His novel *War Horse* has been adapted into an award-winning play and an acclaimed film. From 2003 to 2005, he was the British Children's Laureate, and in 2006 he was awarded an Order of the British Empire. Michael Morpurgo lives on a farm in Devon, England.

MARCUS SEDGWICK established himself as an admired writer of YA fiction alongside a career in publishing; he now writes full-time. He is the author of *Midwinterblood*, which received a Michael L. Printz Award; *Revolver*, which received a Printz Honor; and other acclaimed titles for young adults, as well as his recent first thriller for adults, *A Love Like Blood*. He divides his time between a village near Cambridge, England, and the French Alps.

TANYA LEE STONE was an editor of children's nonfiction for many years before becoming a full-time writer. Her books include the young adult novel *A Bad Boy Can Be Good for a Girl*; the picture books *Elizabeth Leads the Way* and *Who Says Women Can't Be Doctors?*; and the narrative nonfiction titles *Almost Astronauts*, which received a Robert F. Sibert Medal, and *Courage Has No Color*, which received an NAACP Image Award. She lives in Vermont.

Photo by Cathy Bennett

SHEENA WILKINSON has been established as an acclaimed writer for young people since the publication of her multi-award-winning debut novel, *Taking Flight*, which was followed by a sequel, *Grounded*, named the Children's Books Ireland Book of the Year. Her most recent novel, *Too Many Ponies*, is for younger readers. She lives in rural Northern Ireland with a neurotic cat and an ever-increasing book collection.

They shall grow not old,
   as we that are left grow old:
Age shall not weary them,
   nor the years condemn.
At the going down of the sun
   and in the morning
We will remember them.

— Robert Laurence Binyon, "For the Fallen"